HAUTE SURVEILLANCE

HAUTE SURVEILLANCE
JOHANNES GÖRANSSON

TARPAULIN SKY PRESS
GRAFTON, VERMONT
2013

Haute Surveillance
© 2013 Johannes Göransson

Cover art: Fi Jae Lee
        "The Poet Yi Sang's Wedding and Funeral," 2011.
        Fish Skin, Lace, Wire.
        60 x 65 x 153 cm (Yi Sang), 61 x 50 x 178 cm (Yi Sang's Wife)

First Edition, May 2013
ISBN-13: 978-1-939460-00-4
Printed and bound in the USA
Library of Congress Control Number: 2012956045

Tarpaulin Sky Press
P.O. Box 189
Grafton, Vermont 05146
www.tarpaulinsky.com

For more information on Tarpaulin Sky Press perfect-bound and hand-bound editions,
as well as information regarding distribution, personal orders, and catalogue requests,
please visit our website at www.tarpaulinsky.com.

HAUTE SURVEILLANCE

I will always remember the Starlet as a mother remembers a child; or how a father remembers his daughter when he's been tortured in a room for 7 hours; or as a entomologist remembers the different parts of the insect anatomy even when his fingers get too clumsy to dissect a fetal pig.

I remember the Starlet in her fallen state, in a photograph on the third page of the tabloid paper. I remember her in my fallen state of anorexia, in my bang-head while protestors hold up images of complicated bodies in the Shining Mansion on the Hill.

Father Voice-Over tells a story over the PA system. It is the story of how to dissect fetal pigs. He compares them to political prisoners. He declares that the explicit purpose of my slapstick body is obscene. He's wrong. No children can be begotten from sticks.

That's why he loves me.

That's why Mother Machine Gun always carries me through the riots. Why I drink champagne out of her Hiroshima-hands. It tastes like honey but it's sweeter. It makes me nauseous in my entire sticky body.

*

The last time I saw the Starlet she was in a pool. On the news. The shot came from below. She was wearing white pearls. I was wearing white pearls. The last time I saw the Starlet she was a mute girl I had hired to convulse for this explicit purpose: to bring the Starlet back to life. My camera work was sloppy. My crashed-out body was obscene and alarmed in every male part and every infantile spasm.

The reason I used a mute actress was because I am ashamed. Breathing. Bogus. On the verge of a crash-through. Language killed the Starlet. The Starlet did not speak. I don't speak because I am always fainting from hunger. Feed me. Feed me lamb. I'm starving. I starve like actresses with their mouths full of gold. A thousand mute actresses with their mouths full of jewelry.

The mute actress nearly fainted in the video. We talked with our hands: mine were fists, her hands were open. Bang. She was down on the ground. She wore a pretty dress that tore. I wear out the video on which we are down on the ground. Like snakes. Hissing. The microphone breaks halfway through against the actress's body. A blue body. The kind of body that is used to advertise perfume.

★

I write this for the mute actress and the dead girls and the Virgin Father who speaks in this mausoleum and Mother Machine Gun who carries my body through the tumultuous crowds. Sticky and stricken-out, I write this for people on posters. I write this for the breathers and bleeders. I write this with a geometry suggesting awkwardness. I write this as a punishment. I write this for those infested and luxurious and teeming.

I write this for the people who are at war.

*

I write this from hotel rooms and because I have a medical condition. The skin bleeds and pinches. It's a ridiculous death I am living and I live it ridiculously in an economy of trickle-down disease.

Speaking of dead children: Modern architecture makes me nervous.

Speaking of dead children: Sometimes when I listen to the gates of New Jerusalem I think I hear a trapped cat scratching wildly. Other times it is just me. I'm watching a TV show about a trapped cat. It's a sexual act. A slang term. The act involves tattoos and cameras.

Speaking of dead children: There is no place for immigrants in utopia and all film-makers must be renounced. I could never grow up in a house like that. Unless I was a dead child. An embalmed child. A child that never vandalized his own do-wop body with surveillance equipment.

I vandalize my do-wop body due to my modest self-control.

I call my line of work *haute surveillance.*

*

Then why do I look arrested in photographs and absent in drawings?

Insects are pumping their lancets in and out of my sore. It's an almost purple sore. It's a translation. Pornography. A child's drawing. My preferred method of making art involves a torso. The best way to do it is with scissors, said my father in an interview about my pig-killings.

So I write this novel in praise of virgins.

I write this novel in praise of virgins because they are occluded and spectacular.

I write this novel in praise of virgins with strokes.

I write this novel with pig-strokes. In fetal positions. With abortion movements. I write this in praise of virgins with a piece of colored glass.

*

I hate wolves.

I hate femurs.

I hate my body because it's such an infested heap of knickknack.

I hate to see what you have done to my body with the mirror.

I hate mirrors.

I break them and then I get pissed because I feel like Hollywood.

I hate Hollywood for its heap of dead horses.

I hate the way my voice sounds over the PA system in the Shining Mansion on the Hill.

I love my voice when I'm a carcass on the mirror.

*

There are many possible reasons why I ended up in the Shining Mansion on the Hill. Perhaps I was carried by a group of anti-abortion protesters led by Ronald Reagan. Or a man wearing a plastic Reagan mask, which made him sweat. Clouded up his eyes. Perhaps it rubbed off on me. The sweat. The mask. Perhaps the protesters were wearing mutilated costumes. Perhaps they were wearing suits. I was probably an unconscious body, bled and impregnated, stagnant and distant. I was probably dreaming about doing the plug-ugly. I was probably full of shit. Fecal matter. Child decay. Milk teeth.

*

Another explanation: a car accident. The cell phone hit my head. First: absolute silence. Then: Noise. The trees clattered in the wind. An ambulance carried me to America, to the perforation chamber.

*

The Perforation Chamber: The nurse had black nail polish. She sat by my bed and stroked my arms as we watched a documentary about the 1960s. The widow in black looked magical. I told my nurse about my childhood. I told her about how when I laid in between my sleeping parents and kept watch of the door I drew up in my mind fantastic machines to fool our would-be killers – a kind of fake sarcophagus, we would be lowered down beneath our bed, replaced by copies of our sleeping bodies. Life-like copies that would bleed when slashed, emit grunts when kicked. But I worried. If they discovered us beneath our fake bodies we would have no place to run. I didn't tell my nurse that part. It would have upset her. She might have thought I was talking about her metaphorically.

I was talking about the Imagination.

She told me I ought to make movies about my life. And I promised I would.

I would.

It is to that nurse with black nail polish I make this offering of stunt bodies.

*

The expresident claims I was brought to the Shining Mansion on the Hill for drowning the Starlet. He claims it was a jealous rage. That it involved sex and dreams. That we wove our narrative together, that the Starlet and I used black and white photography and a voice-over that explained everything.

It's that voice-over I keep hearing. It explains to us the details of our austere and infested bodies. Including the New Jerusalem we enter into like rats. Including the night body that has several wounds. Including the black body that dances in the midst of mob violence.

The voice-over tells me I am alive like the mob.

The voice-over tells me I live in this Shining Mansion because I made a video of a mute girl in the third world. It is my masterpiece, according to the voice. It is a crime, according to the voice.

According to the voice, even the purest bodies are jerky and the deportations are extreme.

Sometimes when I enter New Jerusalem I enter on a bier or a stretcher or the man with the metals has a swelling. A bloating. There are children in the river. There is a dog that is barking at my genitals. Sometimes when I enter New Jerusalem a woman is holding my penis nonchalantly. It's not a woman. I'm covered with shrapnel.

I'm writing the history of the nation.

*

The sound the body makes is akin to the sound toys make when they burn.

(This is a fantasy I sometimes imagine the way one might imagine one's execution if one made a living injecting poison into beautiful killers and rapists.)

My daughter burns her toys and it smells like the terrorist attack against the towers.

In those towers I keep a picture of a body, a fatso body with staring eyes.

If we're in a strip joint that's the stripper we hope won't come over to our table.

She's the stripper who ruins everything.

I'm getting into character.

For the Sensation.

*

We still live in a war economy. I make movies with a war economy. You read case histories with a war economy. I make war movies about perforations and proliferation. You are soundproof you are war-proof you are surveillance footage. I am blunted out. My language is so counterfeit I must have cancer. I must have a glass staff with a little beak at the tip.

But I don't want to give you the impression that I'm a nihilist. I'm a moralist of the zero mouth.

I'm writing this memoir in praise of virgins.

I'm placing a flower in a mute girl's belly.

A flower taken from the corrupted body of a bludgeoned child. I don't know what the flower is called but it looks like a curled-up fetus. I write this novel as one would write a word on a fetus.

*

This novel is dedicated to the people who shoot bodies.

*

Father Voice-Over sings to me in the dark while I listen to bodies being shot at. While I read the latest reports from the riots by the blue bomb light that I dedicate to stunt doubles. For they refuse transcendence. They refute my future. They refute my significance. In their novels I finally bleed out.

I interpret the dresses of victims. They tell me how to find my way out of the riots.

This novel is written like a fashion show dedicated to the rioted body.

This novel is based on a vision I had in 1991. In the middle of a riot. It was a counterfeiters riot and I was passing out from drugs. The singer sang a song about boredom and I was leveled with a punch. Our Mother of the Machine Gun picked me up and carried me through the mute melee.

*

Our Mother of the Machine Gun: The reason you don't like the war is because you're not in it.

*

Our Son Drained and Exhausted: The reason you don't love Our Mother is because you're not being petted with a silver bullet.

*

When I'm petted by a nurse, when I'm having my blood drawn I inevitably imagine new fashions for immigrants. A bicyclist will find me in the morning. The ads will be exposed to the snow. The tag line will be: "Feel at home, screamer."

The sales will be overwhelming.

I go to my high-school friend's funeral and put a postcard in the coffin: "Wish you were here in the belly of the slaughtered whale."

He goes to my funeral and leaves a note that says: "You weren't here, you didn't see anything."

*

Question: Who the fuck isn't a foreigner here? Aren't we all immigrants? Aren't we all from somewhere else? Don't we all relate?

Answer: Watch the movies. Read the subtitles. Can you tell which one is the foreigner? It's the one with the horrible mice-sounds. But the subtitles read: "Pleased to meet you, Sir. I've brought you a gift from my homeland."

*

Question: Do foreigners always film themselves with tacky plastic video cameras?

Question: Do foreigners know how fantasize like bling blong blang?

Question: Has a foreigner ever asked you for direction out of the mess room?

Question: Have you ever shot a foreigner?

*

All of the foreigners were shot because of their incestuous relationships on the set. It was a horrible set: the blowtorch looked tacky and the walls were too soft. I don't ever want to go back there to see what happened in the heat and the way the confetti got so wet and the skin was so yucky. I was so blond, I was your brother.

*

All of *The Shining* was shot with sets. The snow was salt. It was 110 degrees inside the soundstage. The air was saturated with gasoline fumes. The cameramen and camerawomen wore gas-masks as the ran through the rooms chasing the little boy. There were antennae in the walls. The production crew built up an entire hotel inside. Nothing was fake.

*

It was The Real Thing.

*

That is what I have always wanted to create. The first time I got close was with *In the Penal Colony* because I made it with a stick and a stone and an orchestra of genius children.

But I got even closer with a mute girl and my ki-ko-pee body.

My prettiest trousers were down along my ankles and my scotch-guard crown fell on the ground.

This is how we reproduce a ki-ko-pee body: every mouth must bite, every eye must hurt, every spasm must infect the image.

That's what they say on TV.

Also, they say I'm a moron for the way I went along with the Starlet's experiments with ki-ko-pee bodies.

*

The Parable of the Ki-Ko-Pee Body: People have accused me of plagiarizing my films. The parables must have been created by a teenage girl, my accusers say. A girl with a cutting disorder or a virgin with fantasies of the Third World. Or an anorexic.

This is the first lesson in haute surveillance: Always write like you're a teenage virgin.

Always reach for the gun.

Gasoline, cannibalism and sweets

Do you own this place? Did you invent it for the Cancer?

Today I cleaned my cadaver and painted the nails red.

An homage to patricide.

A stalemate in Grand Hotel Chasm.

Grind Hotel.

*

"The Black Night of Godlessness"

(A smelly smouldering wick is left behind.)

*

The expresident arrived with an obscene machine. In the middle of a protest. The machine is stuck to his throat and it speaks through his cancer: feeble ideas about love. Through this machine he predicts evacuations and mimery, kidnappings and dance lessons.

He tells me jokes about my body. He says: There are places where babies burn because a certain kind of jelly is applied to their skin.

The presidency, he says, was much like a disease. This Shining Mansion on the Hill is like a vacation or Literature, he says. He says it with a grave voice. The presidency, he says was so real it almost broke him down. It almost broke me down, he says and looks at his shivering hands. With these hands I killed live swans, he says and looks at me.

*

There are many reasons why the expresident's antibody was brought here on a bier. He thinks it is because the children burned inside buildings. Bombed buildings. Art. Sand. Femur-strands. The looted museum of his memory. All of it continues to burn.

He thinks it's on account of his wife, who wants me to teach Art to the shellshocked soldiers.

*

I think it's because of the economy.

What are you talking about, says the expresident.

A bunch of shit, I admit. Whenever someone says it's the economy, they're talking about Art.

You were brought here for Art, I tell him.

*

The expresident entered the White House on a bone-white Horse, tooting a silver trumpet, but he will not personify death in this tale for he is not yet ridiculous enough. I will try to make him more ridiculous but I will fail and fail because only by constantly losing can we have the kind of beauty that will be sufficiently flimsy. Like death. Or soundtracks. Only by suffering in an exhaustion of flowers and bodily discolorations can we have a cashed beauty equal to the saturation that surrounds us.

Nor will the corporate grinners with their wigs and blue shirts personify death.

My Starlet will personify death.

She will personify death as she sits in her pool chair wearing a blue bikini, her body starved and her eyes beautiful. She will personify death as she lazily handles my penis in the remake of catastrophes with sloppy camera work. In the waning days of the deadly administration, the Starlet will personify death and I will be represented by pop songs about cocaine.

*

Culture is a taxidermy museum but the horses are beautiful and the letter openers disinfected.

The cum on my face tickles as I type these pages out.

*

The Foreigner Body: Must be entered into the pageant as objects to be classified and quantified. And it must be banged up.

Banged. Bang. That was the sound of a door. The foreigner's body must be a door. It must be shot with the finest surveillance equipment. It must be shot. It must be numb with cum.

*

I love Kleist

*

When the guards asked me all those questions (Is your body a faggot? Do you speak radio? Why are your spasms so infantile? What would happen if we pulled this plastic bag off your head? How is your wham-blam-dunk?) I could barely make out what they said. I denied everything, not because I liked hearing my voice underwater, but I knew that was what the kidnappers wanted me to say. They loved the way I said No. They could listen to me say No all day long and far into the night. This was a test. They knew I was up to the task at hand. They even removed the bag from my head.

*

I don't want to defend abortions on moral grounds.

I believe in abortions because I believe in Art.

When the nurse and I watched the black widow walking in a funeral march, I could hear the nurse breathing.

She looked magical.

This book is for my nurse.

But the eyes are for the widow.

The Widow Party: I wrote a play called *The Widow Party*. It was performed at Links Hall in Chicago last May. It's about two widows – one black and one white. The black one speaks through a little tape-player she carries on her chest, the white one was played by Patrick D. He gets killed over and over. To get his act right we wrapped his penis in cellophane. The black widow was played in black-face by Jen K., who recently collected the favorite sayings of all the soldiers dead in Iraq. My favorite one is "at the end of the day a wreck is still just a girl." It came from an army doctor from Memphis, TN. My second favorite was "You love your country like you love your dog. When it's over you bury it in the backyard and pray that the badgers will keep out." That one came from a young man from Sunflower, MS. That's a town in which I drink champagne out of my mother's hands. My black mother who bleeds. My white mother who treats me with shards and shakes me tonight as I enter into New Jerusalem on a stolen horse.

*

There's no greater cliché than a soldier masturbating into a glass of champagne. There is no greater cliché than a mother.

*

I have seen the photographs the Starlet took. They have been circulating over the Internet and handed around at protests. There is the footage of the naked man being bit by dogs, the image of the heap of naked man piled into a pyramid, the footage of a man with a hood over his head and electrical wires strapped to his hands, the image of the man with a Disney mask on his face and on his genitals, the image of a woman puking into a meat hell. I think I know why but I'm not telling. *Atrocity kitsch.*

*

All the students claim they have brothers or sisters or uncles who's been to the war and when they return they try to strangle their spouses at night in their sleep. It appears the war is connected to the bedroom in a cliché way. But those pathetic sprawling bodies in the dark: those are the bodies with which I want to populate this skin flick.

*

There are so many soldiers in the mansion that they have been given a room of their own. It's a large room but there are so many soldiers that they have to cram them in on small cots. They're here to be decontaminated, to have the violence from the theater of war rinsed off them like swans. It's not going so well. It seems every day a soldier kills another soldier with some sharp object. I've been instructed to teach them how to write poetry in order to direct their violence to something more constructive. Father Voice-Over doesn't realize that Art is a Violence. And vice versa. There is already so much Art in these muscular bodies, I cannot prevent them from expressing it.

*

Tonight I want to make a movie about skin.

Decoy skin.

I want to make it for the enemy.

To lure him out.

*

I can't hear a thing in here.

*

Media makes stunt doubles.

This poem for example is about mine.

He wears a wig to his assassination.

The erotics of writing reminds me of the needle on a record player.

*

Of all the movies I made with the Starlet, my favorite was our mumble-version of *Hiroshima Mon Amour*. Or the Jacobean piece we filmed in a shooting range. The clothes I wore were positively repulsive by the time she was finished with me. My body was covered with wax. I played the part of the wax figures. She played the part of the slaughter. It was also a mumble movie. It was hard to hear anything in the ricochet.

*

Miss World: This novel is a spell, but I can't help it if this novel turns into a pile-up of disgusting bodies and glorifications of black-outs.

*

Whenever I come to the soldiers' barrack, they are engaged in some kind of art production: bodies in fetal lamb poses for example, or snuff videos of daddy, ouch-ouch-it-hurts, corny dances (like the hostage crisis, the twist, the pork out, the pile up, the photographs). They love to wear Mickey Mouse masks when they hurt each other like children. Don't pork me up, Mickey, I hear one man cry as I slam the door. I can't help them, I can just hope to contain them. I need to keep them apart from the anti-abortion protestors and the actors. Swine hunt! Swine hunt! I hear from the inside as I swiftly lock the door.

*

The expresident wants every body naked. And he wants no sound. It should be deaf in here, he says, and then he points out that there are stains on my clothes and that the letter opener is making an awful racket in my mouth. I'm a dangerous man when I get around the wrong instruments. Milk and blood, milk and blood, I think to myself. It's always this way after a riot.

*

I can't help it if I begin to breathe funny or look funny or hit myself in the face.

This I the fault of language.

Language is like candy. It rots my teeth. It makes me spazzy.

That's why I love skin-flicks: the way they pile all those porno bodies up. Ugly bodies. The skin color demented by video. In pornos we're all foreigners, or at least tourists. Everything is Art. Especially the Skin!

*

My wife's skin and hair get darker every day. Wearing an oriental veil, she tells me about total wrecks. It may seem archaic to be talking about those kinds of bodies in this day and age of drones flying across the desert, but these bodies hold a symbolic importance to me because I approach the world as through an apocryphal travelogue. Below deck, in the dark, the insect-like bodies struggle to breathe, the travelogue tells me. Treat skinny bodies as you would a murderer or a victim. Don't let them out of your sight. My wife does not belong in this mansion, though she was born here. She cannot leave without me and our daughter. I can't leave. I'm not allowed.

*

And I'm not allowed to stray too far away from the anti-abortion protesters.

*

I hold a large, blue opium flower at the protest.

*

The expresident is redundant from power.

*

The main passage is dead from children.

*

The Genius Child Orchestra: It is not entirely clear how the orchestra was assembled. It seems to have emerged from the war. Something about the embedded television imagery must have given rise to a taste for their death-like tutti-frutti music. It's not clear how many of them there are. They appear to be parasites. Their songs seem to be invariably rewrites of other people's songs. The first song of theirs I heard I heard on the day the Starlet died. It was a song about swimming pools made of cattle bones. It was dedicated to the Starlet. I've heard they live in the Shining Mansion on the Hill. Their new song is about a haunted house. They must be patricidal.

*

Together we are working in a new medium: sweat cloths. We're interested in mediumicity. In one sweat cloth we see an image of an artist's body after a car crash: all ornamental. In another we see a dark lady who may be our lady of video malaise. In another we see a word: woundability. In the fourth one we see our lady of the machine guns after the parade, all slack and messy.

*

How can you trust a woman with such black hair, asks the expresident about my wife. I don't trust her, I say, I love her. She's given me a black flower and painted black drops across my face and torso.

*

I always knew the starlet had a cunt. And I suspected that her cunt was twisted like a whelk, that it tasted like a whelk, that it felt like a whelk. That is what everyone was thinking on that day many years ago when she refused to come out of her trailer to act in her comeback role. It was ridiculous.

When I watched the drama unfold. When I saw the Starlet's trailer from the helicopter's point of view, I realized I must be a virgin. But not the kind of virgin that is a concussion. Or that has never been photographed by foreigners. I was the kind of virgin that has no eyes. Or whose eyes have been put on display.

*

When I saw her dead in the pool I realized I must be a virgin with a whelk for a heart.

*

Sometimes virginity is a state, like concussion or starvation.

Other times it's a visual phenomenon.

The world looks clean and violent.

A foreigner is always a perverted virgin.

Throw the foreigner's body in the backseat.

Have you ever worked at a meat plant?

Watch me read the messy transcriptions.

*

The ambulance instruments all have interesting names: the respirator, the vandalized victim, the chair, the childish torso, the stable, the fake, the insides of a smashed virgin, the squeals, the corrupt flower, the daughter, the burn victim, the copy machine, the kinomutilator, the fetus camera, the underwear, the Japanese insect system and the Whale. I love the butterfly collection. It's what they use on the soldiers.

*

The Great Voice-Over does not want to show me at my most brutal and belligerent. The street is indeed littered with bodies he has had to get rid of but he does not want to let me out. The last time I met The Great Voice-Over was at a movie about the female body, about its crevices and cancers. No the heroine does not die. That was me slumped over in the corner. I was hungry and maybe strangled. Mostly I was anorexic.

*

Ignore the subtitles

*

My wife has a photograph of me on the wall. She took it with a camera I once threw at a model. It's a picture of me from behind and my skin looks disheveled. She once told me she had licked the film she used, licked it with her mouth full of thorns. She tells me she wants to take a photograph of me with a black plastic bag full of flowers. I tell her that won't work, you'll need a hole to let the light in. You will be my camera, she says.

*

Dark Satanic Mills sound like pianos, my arms sound like la la la.

Samarkand.

*

The expresident tells me to watch the news reports about the black man who escaped from his own trial. It sounds like he was putting on a performance in that trial, says the expresident. Like he said, 'these are my arms, my legs, my severed penis, my burnt hair, my millions of seed dripping from the trees, my million bugs swarming around.' I agree, it sounds like a performance, or more like an anti-performance, or a performance that is bound to fail. Which is art, according to my wife. The expresident seems excited, remembering something about his own life that he won't reveal to the rest of us. Perhaps he's thinking about using a rifle to kill deer, like in the old poems. Perhaps he's thinking about the wars he loved to describe in theatrical terms. Perhaps he's thinking about the inflation crisis that follows art wherever it goes (wars, trials, mansions).

*

I'm thinking about a Langston Hughes poem about shriveled up fruit covered in flies. About a box of flies. My torso: The inflation crisis of the photographed body. I'm getting it ready. For the Sensation.

*

The Sensation: I tell the expresident that I want to hurt a rich person and he's the only rich person I know. He calls in the guards. A week later he hugs me and we make up when they let me out of the cage. I want to get back in the cage. Or I want my body to be a cage. I want to let you out. I want to lock you out. Incredible.

*

In all of this a voice keeps telling me we're in Spokane.

*

explicate, infiltrate, media

*

On television: A black man surprises the guards at his own trial, ripping the gun from one of them and mowing down both the judge and the guard before stealing a car and taking off into the city. This story is all over the television, on every channel, and the expresident is fascinated. I think the Genius Child Orchestra could write a song about him, something about his jacket, the cut, helicopters. I could sing it in blackface in front of a tableau inspired by lynchings. This could be seen as a form of homosexuality. Or a kind of Fame.

*

The Dilemma of Father Voice-Over: Nobody can hear him talking. They think they're hearing themselves think.

*

One day I peek into the soldiers' ward and they're all making cod pieces out of egg cartons while drinking Cristal.

The soldiers tell me: We don't want these fashions to end, we just want to burn our effigies while wearing them, and we want to wear the hood when we feel fancy and we want to wear the emaciation like we belong here, the hospital of innocence, the drag-out softcore Together we have built out of a rubbled nation with a lot of money.

*

In The Penal Colony: If this script is ever to be performed I hope it will be performed as a travesty, a snuffing. The voice-over should be done by a newscaster while wearing a rose in his bellybutton. The audience will never see the flower but it will be taken from the corrupted body of a child. I'm an expert on flowers. And the anatomies of fetuses.

In The Penal Colony: I make a point of always being television-horny when I make my films out of discarded gasoline documentaries women's farces faces sticks. This is how the cattle culture becomes mute with wonders and my inside becomes the emulsification of ganglia and the children are children of bankers. In another age this would be the state that would represent salvation. In our culture we don't have a word for it but we hope it will end and that the music will be awesome and suicide.

Everyday people tell stories about the average inmate as if we were all suffering from the same disease in general. We are but lets pretend we're soldiers.

*

"The Smashed Virgin" is easy to forget. It's where the fashion shows go wrong. It's where the protesters learn how to act. It's where the victims learn how to scream. I've always felt that that's where I belonged. Not here, with the plague experts.

*

There are rumors that the Black Man who escaped from his own trial was a soldier back from the war, that he had caught the violence there and could not clean it off himself. It is rumored that he killed his wife and covered her with silk. He poured melted lead over her face. He's retinal in his violence. He makes me want to write poetry. About video and hair. These are two subject matters I care a lot about. I only write about things that fascinate me.

*

The brilliant thing about Jean-Michel Basquiat's paintings is the way the canvas looks like skin, the way the paint looks like bodily fluids and secretions. The skin as medium. No more medium purity. It's already a body.

*

corruptible saints

*

syphilitic orgies in deserted movie sets

*

Helter Skelter

*

race wars

*

The expresident tells me about a vision he had repeatedly during the waning days of his administration. He says it felt like Paris at the fall of Vichy, where young boys and lepers languished on rooftops with rifles, enthralled with death's spasmodic beauty.

*

The expresident says in the dream he was taking care of a baby when suddenly there were three no four babies and he was trying to rinse them by hand but soon there were five or six and then he had to start strangling them he strangled and he strangled but they just grew more numerous and louder and then he woke up from his wife scratching his face. He had tried to strangle her in the dream and she was scratching him in her dream.

In her dream she was young again and in love with someone she had read about in a book, someone who took her in a car and the light burned out everything. It was the desert. Everything burned out the desert.

*

Burn out the desert

Burn out every socket and every transparent dress

*

We watch recreations of the Black Man's escape from the court room. The actors and actresses are amateurs, and they speak their lines in a stilted way that both my wife and I find lovely. We hate realism but we know it's oppressive.

The expresident says: the blood looks fine, but the bleeding is too fake.

In other words, he's afraid of what will happen if every event can be seen as Art. But this is all we immigrants want. It would be an acknowledgement.

*

It seems like this hospital is understaffed. I'm not only playing the patient, I am also injecting and inhaling. I am pretending that the children are anesthetized as we build up a symbolic relationship between body and voice that we will tear down in one messy dissection. But that hasn't happened yet. There is still a voice-over.

There is a black body for every disease, a hygiene for every central tenet of our impotent rage.

*

My secret diary: There are pages torn out.

The rides are too rickety.

I chew gum but I know it won't help my genitals.

I use a stingray in the cutting room but the staplers don't work on my skin.

Only silver bullets take.

*

People always seem to want to warn me. A ballet instructor tells me to be on my guard against white people, especially soldiers:

they will steal the silver out of your veins. What none of them seem to understand is that I've been in every porn shop of this damned penal colony. I've blacked out at the rock n' roll shows devoted to death. I've read through the manuals: burn-victims, breathalyzers, see-through garments, starvation celebration.

*

Together with some drive-by victims and some extras I have perfected the violent art of looking nailed on television.

I wrote this novel in praise of virgins because they look *nailed on TV.*

*

The soldiers' naked bodies seem to have a certain lustre to them, as if they were on TV, or covered with a shiny liquid. One woman comes crying, shaking, pleading with me to wipe her body clean. It is covered with a silver paint, which makes me think about the Starlet. I get the silver all over my hands and it strikes me that it might contaminate my skin so I move away from her, but she follows me to the door, pleading and shaking. I won't see her again

*

The Slop Chamber: I'm learning my new voice.

Voice-Over: I look the part of the exhibitor.

*

"A Self-Attack in 13 Frames"

A Kino-Mutilation for Gorged Pigs

*

The whistle-dogs will not stop

They too can smell the slop hole

*

I like the expresident's interpretation of the rape scene in *Blue Velvet*: Frank is trying to bring Dorothy Valens out of her numbness, back to life. This is what art does. It takes us out of the suburbs, it makes us into peeping toms, it creates maniacs out of our kitschy safe homes and then it forces us to shoot them through the head. But most of all it creates a dance to pull us away from the Void, a muted television. We're down on all fours with our gas masks on, convulsing for the blank woman.

*

Today I got a letter from an exgirlfriend who accused me of having killed the Starlet. "This has you written all over it," she wrote. "For one, your love of swimming pools, and two, your hatred of women's bodies." She could never figure out that I loved her body, didn't hate it. She loved fur and kept a guinea pig in her closet. After sex I would hear that thing scuffle around, chewing on cardboard. She hated her guinea pig. I loved her guinea pig.

*

blood on the key boards
blood on the key boards

*

Sometimes during my epileptic attacks, I flail and knock over my ink container, causing black black ink to cover over my sheets of poetry. My wife holds up the dripping sheets to the window and reads them. She uses her occult genius expertly when it comes to my body. She pours the ink on my torso and writes something with the sharp end of a compass. An illegible dedication.

*

Sometimes when I'm melancholy the expresident draws a smile on my face with lipstick. Except it's not a smile. Not even lipstick. Sometimes he crams my throat full of fois gras. It makes me want to vomit. All that liver paste in my mouth. Makes me want to write emails to girls telling them I'm sorry that I punched them in the face or the belly. But I don't. I chew the liver and look out the window. The teenagers are being disgusting with their bodies again.

*

I love my wife because she is soft.

We look so good together and we will marry you.

We are underground. We are underground.

*

My wife must be played by a man, judging from the way she likes to smash.

*

Today on the news they say the Black Man murders children because his own children were killed by soldiers. They say you can hear him breathe when he's close. I can hear insects when my daughters are close. I can hear the economy in my soldiers. I can hear the hyena on the TV. The expresident is watching one of the Starlet's movies again. It's the one about civil war again. I play the part of "inflation" with a rose in my mouth and pigs at my feet. Love poetry for the 21st century.

*

The partisans, anorexic in funereal poses, tell me that there is an overwhelming virginity to the riots. The participants remain on the whole pure in their visual frenzy.

The real cameraman is tied up and muffled like queers or horses or horse thieves who are hanged or emaciated daughters who take their place in the sensationalistic black.

The victim is not like the body my nurse held like a beautiful but dying horse. He was more like a copy. He smells like spermicide. Especially his fingers, which have been broken.

*

Sometimes it happens that I have a thorn. I try to pull it out but certain administrators feel it's important that I keep it in. Without that thorn I may go on to become Arsonist or a Dictator Who Loves Art. If I were a Dictator who Loved Art I would commission mostly heaps and heaps of hot sand because my fondest memories are of being a child laying in the hot sand watching the women strut around. This is too ridiculous according to the administration to represent true nostalgia.

*

The pornography should not come until later.

*

I'm starving but I can't stop watching the recreations of the Black Man's escape. My wife slips "crookies" in my coffee.

*

The Dilemma of Father Voice-Over: Who has put up all these posters on the walls? They appear to be made of glass and the pornographic content is nacreous.

The Dilemma of Father Voice-Over: He tends to give me messages meant for girls: where to cut, how to hurt like insects, when to start the footage of the infection. When I complain to the rabid woman next to me she flings herself against me. I lick her tits.

Meanwhile the voice-over has moved on to more pressing matters: burn victims, cosmetics, black-outs, how to tent a wound, how to copulate a thriving.

Fathers candy all things over.

By the time I am a-cumming into the girl's smack-cunt the voice is speaking most gravely about things that most definitely has to do with the assassination body at hand: perforations, lye, a crawl that needs to be killed, porcelain. It is no surprise when the nurses begin to shave my body. I have seen it all before in a dream I dreamt five minutes before in typography.

I'm with Alice all the way.

Children eat sweet meats.

*

I have a fever. A young Asian woman – utterly without plastic or pubic hair – has brought me an old-fashioned phonograph, on which she plays an old standard about the moraine fish. The woman makes a high-pitched wail. She opens her hand: insect antennae. I can feel the blood trickling down my lips I can hear the crunch. I am too weak to spit. She spits for me.

*

(soft music)

It's hard to pull the plug. Somewhere a killer is whiter than the makeup I wear to sleep in the underground. And a lover is devouring nectarines while his penis glows.

I have a metallic exhaustion but I'm perfecting the instruments. On the radio my wife is picking up the sounds of scabby peonies and fetus lilies. "The birds," she says, "are father birds, thrashing around in the hole."

The ampoules are empty.

I have a skinned animal as my sign.

I smile. I'm anorexic. It's really happening.

I am busy prepping the scratch-up figures for the stagger. Deep inside my clit of a heart I can feel the egregious nature of random bodies.

*

The soldiers have involved me in an exercise to exorcise violence from their bodies. It's beautiful but it does not feel good in one's body. I do not know why they associate my body in particular with death. I am not a serial killer. The expresident could be said to be a serial killer, but he plays a virginal, almost child-like role in the exercise. He welcomes an invasion with his body. I welcome a riot with my carnation body. My wife says my outbreak.

*

There can be no voice-over in dark matter. The computer's voice-over has been removed from the original. While both versions are about film, the first version is more about an atomic fear, the second one is the fear of cancer and proliferating terror attacks.

I make up my own voice-over, which should be whispered as if somebody was kicking you in the ribs. I make up a voice-over about make-up, which I like to wear to the penetrations. But I realize that's a ridiculous and self-defeating thing to do because most of all I want to be submerged in dark matter. Almost drowned. Almost covered in jizz.

*

The Dilemma of Women's Voices: The women voices are numberless and yet we cannot hear them for all the background shouts and a woman in sequin tries to chant a war song but we fuck she bites hard the leather strap she says: Do the voice over, do the voice over, you anorexic fuck.

*

My wife studies the effects of contamination on bugs.

*

The expresident wants to know why my wife is so frequently watching movies about Ivan the Terrible. Everytime I look into her room I see flames and beautiful clothes, flames and beautiful clothes, flames and beautiful clothes.

*

In a black-and-white fashion shoot in the desert, the Starlet appears empty-eyed, almost hollow. She is dirty. She is in the sand with a bearded man and their birds are dirty like rats and the rats are crawling on the Starlet's body. This was when the Starlet was at the height of her Fame and Beauty. This is when she was so beautiful it was like rabies all over. Autism. There was no voice-over that told us about the effects of the medicine. That would come later like a body count. Like the Road to Joy, it is littered with bodies.

*

In the palace of wisdom, the bodies are numbered with a charcoal pen.

*

I like to watch movies in an empty swimming pool. That this pool was made of cattle bones only makes the situation more special. According to the film the pool was built on the site of a native american burial ground but none of us believe this.

There is something curiously wrong with my mouthpiece. The porcelain has browned and the exoskeleton is soured. My face looks scared as if I were playing the part of a plague victim in a cabaret number from Weimar Germany. I can't make out the snatch.

*

Someone tells me I have infants or infant-shock and something has to be done about the cysts.

*

When the schoolchildren ask me I tell them I'm here because I shot a starlet. They know I'm telling the truth because they have seen my picture on the assassination channel but we all pretend I'm lying and I give them some candy that actually belongs to my ex-girlfriend, the molested child of an army vet. I've kept it all this time because I felt it must be a symbol of the dangers of childhood but now it all makes sense to me again.

The sores in my head are acting up, bleeding. I keep rubbing my forehead and it turns my hands red or strangely orange the ganglia is irritated my eyes look smiled.

You are not here. I am pretty in my torso and with my strangely carny voice. It says: Come back to cattle seizures.

rat out

arsonist

kerosene, mon amour

*

My favorite number is the one in which the girl with the pained expression sings "come on get happy" so slowly I think I can see her snatch when she bends over but I'm not sure it's so dark in here. She sure knows how to wear carnations in epidemic zones. I call her Mother of the Machine Gun because of the way she wipes the sweat off her forehead and the way she carries me in the Jacobean tragedy in which I get hurt in the head. Ouch. Ouch.

*

The soldiers want to know the real truth about the Black Man, they tell me. I tell them I don't know any more than they do. They get violent. I dance for them with my shirt over my head. They ask if they too can contact him.

*

I want us all to wear kimonos. And sharp swords. And at some point we cut ourselves open. Just the hearts sitting there throbbing in our open body cases. The children would look a lot like us, dear film-maker, I think to myself as I see them carry in a man who looks nauseatingly beautiful, tricked out and barely alive. He's from the war, I'm informed. The war against terrorism or the war against the body. Both. We'll welcome him with milk and blood.

*

Where are you?

I need to practice my new role on you it's the ventriloquist in the show about jews. You know the one in which they decapitate a little white boy.

*

I have a hand that goes click-click and an arm and a torso that crinkles and a mouth that can be filled with sound, but I'm suspicious of this memory. It seems perhaps to have been planted in my mind by Marxist theorists who want there to be such a place as home. I had a concussion, not a home.

*

Speaking of silent cinema: My wife is getting fatter and fatter. She is with child again, a child we will name after the Underworld, Nico.

*

Sometimes the body on the screen looks so disgusting, sometimes so beautiful: it's what the Starlet loved about cinema, and why she would have loved the images of the Black Man. Once she told me I cared too much about being beautiful as she placed a horned crown on my head. "Now wipe the blood from your forehead," she whispered from behind her beautiful, shiny camera.

*

When I watch a road movie, I wonder how they get rid of all the hair, how to make the body that smooth and uninfected. They should hire the costume designers for the "Smashed Virgin." They could do wonders over there. Later I almost devour my wife, licking her every orifice with my tongue. My tongue is idiotic. It's not my mother tongue, it's my idiot tongue. Moron tongue. Even while fucking, foreigners are in road movies. Kitsch. Kill them all.

*

Save modernism

*

from its own corpses

*

I used to be a butcher but that was before subtitles.

*

It's bad luck to use a gun against an image, says the occultist who does not think I should have killed the movie star. But at least you did it in a swimming pool.

He loved her too, he says but he says that while drinking a glass of champagne.

To Hiroshima! he exclaims suddenly.

To Images! I reply.

There are asian girls on the television they are wearing intricate outfits it looks like the clothes were made for a masque of some kind perhaps the masque of the maternal voice. I fear they will be eaten through by worms. That is what happens to pop stars who look like that.

They become realistic.

*

I watch a film: Hello, I am Gilad, son of Noam and Aviva Shalit, brother of Hadas and Yoel, who lives in Mitzpe Hila. My ID number is 300097029. As you see I am holding in my hands the Palestine newspaper of Sept. 14, 2009, published in Gaza. I am reading the paper in order to find information regarding myself, hoping to find some information from which I would learn of my release and upcoming return home. I have been hoping and waiting for the day of my release for a long time. I hope the current government will not waste the chance to finalize a deal, and I will therefore be able to finally have my dream come true and be released. I will now walk up to the camera to show to you that my body is intact. One of the women that were exchanged for this video just gave birth to her ninth child.

"The heat, pappa, is killing us!"

Fantasies of the Maternal Voice: As I noted in another book I went to the riots to find my mother. I still don't understand fire arms or pet arms but I know how to break into a clinic. That is where I found my Mother of the Machine Gun. I wasn't there.

I didn't see anything, said the voice-over repeatedly.

I rehearsed with thinner at least forty times in the dark we were allowed to speak with accents but I had noseblood on my pillow this morning. That was the second fantasy of the maternal voice and it was more difficult than the first one and very much based on court procedures against illegals.

And who is the scariest in this entire haunted house?

Me of course.

Me and my ssssssturbations.

In the latest reports from the war, all the killers are decorated with flowers and all the victims have crushed seeds in their eyes. All of Baghdad smells so sweetly, says the Viceroy into the microphone, a trilobite with strings attached. The victims are all black from fire. The photographs are all black from sex. I'm blacking out the murder instruments with my fingers dipped in ink. I'm going to burn the reports or scatter them like confetti. The Viceroy suspects that the corpses in the street are a sign that there's a serial killer on the loose in Baghdad.

*

I learn how to use my knife to apply the proper dose of strychnine. I learn from the children. They learn with the television blaring bodiesbodies.

*

bodiesbodiesbodiesbodies

*

Sssstrubations

Ssssturbarrrtionssss

*

I have horses that are infected and girl singers who hyacinth me while I hurt stuffed animals. It's a hallucination to have such a strokey relationship to one's knife-girl.

Here I am staring at my ceiling for probably a half hour while the world all rabbles up and the museums are looted and looted and looted and all the urns and knives and razorblades are pulled out and in and out and the best part of *The Shining* is when Shelley Duvall is running down the stairs and she sees those two guys in furry outfits that's when she may lose it may become an artist instead of a mother.

That hotel is built on bones.

This hotel is built on microphones.

The problem with microphones is that they are attached to the body and picks up all the sounds: the skin, scratches, pearls, kisses, hisses teeth, looking, gasoline, trilobites, ornamentations, Hiroshima, tape crackling, insect crawls, ashes. It's an arrival we are looking for, not just another way out. It's a deportation we deserve for our botched models.

*

Lets kill ourselves a son?

I only have daughters.

(I can't hear a thing in here.)

I have a nightmare about a girl covered with blood and when I wake up sweating my wife tells me a fairytale. It begins with a girl who finds a bleeding raven in the woods and the raven promises the girl it will give her a wish if she saves him so she runs through the woods, covered with blood while the raven cries and cries. The girl reaches her dad and tells him, "Save it, save it, Dad, and it will make one of my wishes come true." But the dad tells her that the raven has rabies – "Look at those opaque, blue, evil eyes" – and cuts its throat with a knife. The next morning when the girl wakes up, she runs to her door and outside of the door she finds a beautiful but simple dark, wood box. Inside she finds a golden axe with which to kill her father. But instead of sneaking upstairs and decapitating her father as instructed, she walks into the forest to look for the raven and in the woods she meets many many children, all of them looking for the raven with sharp objects in their hands. As soon as they find any animal, they murder it brutally – including birds, but also horses and squirrels. Soon they are covered in blood and screaming. Horrified, the girl returns home. She finds the door ajar. Calls her dad. Nobody answers. She tiptoes up the stairs to his room and finds his pale, dead body covered with black feathers. She runs back to the children in the woods but it's too late. By the time she gets there they are already attacking each other atrociously. Somewhere the raven sings its ugly ugly song.

The Soldiers are making a morality play about the Black Man, who brings the plague into the city. He travels with an acting troop. Though at times it seems that he's been taken hostage. The actors are in search of "wonder blood" and that's their downfall. I have "you're it" written on my ribcage. The whole performance is a marriage of technology and puberty.

*

Nothing says glamour like a woman with a half-dead man by her side. And glamour is the loss of meaning, according to Father Voice-Over.

Everything my wife touches ruins the allegory. My penis for example is now meaningless.

The camera is on.

I make a spasmodic pose for the penal colony. It is meant to teach morality Although nobody is supposedly ever let out of their cages.

*

I've heard the most bodiesbodies are piled up in the wing of the mansion called the Smashed Virgin. They are maybe trannies attacked on the street for impersonating themselves. I've heard the ugliest animals are kept in the wing called The Childish Torso. I've heard the women are all naked in the Burn Victim. But the worst rumors are the ones I've heard about my own bodies. These often involve Polaroid cameras. Look: my hand, my eye, a pile of children's shoes, a burning oil rig, a taxidermied white horse, inside a museum, it sounds like winter organs. We are finished, mock epic, bogus-bled, shit.

*

I need to fine-tune my instruments. My daughters always come back. Reproduced.

*

They have pig strokes.

I have sunstrokes.

I wear a gas mask for the finale.

The finale: My father's mansion has many exit wounds.

Our Lady of the Strangest Victim: Nothing was fake.

*

I'm so hungry it's like I was throbbing oriental fluids. The effect is ornithological. The material is bodies. A thousand bogus bodies.

*

According to one breaking report, the Black Man is assuming all kinds of disguises. The most recent: an out-of-work actor who smells like shit. No, the most recent: a woman who cannot put out a fire. No: a child of art. No: Art.

My glass leg is getting worse. I tell the girl to stop but she can't hear me. She's almost dead. Almost the real thing.

*

The soldiers are not getting less artful. Everytime I venture into their barracks they're partying with the equipment and photographing each other in painful poses they claim are inspired from Arabian Nights. I don't know. It looks like those poses are from America. At least "the screwy doll." Americans love dolls and they love to eat.

*

My wife turns on my favorite movie about Father Voice-Over. Black and White. The treasures literally pour over the bodies. He's getting married. What a farce. What a cold war farce.

Where are the spies?

I could compare Father Voice-Over's moustache in this film to a cockroach because my daughter loves cockroaches. She refers to sleep as "cockroaches." She loves to sleep. Sometimes she is out for several days. The PA emits a lullaby. In it the child is called "Winter." "Winter," sings the Father, "will last until spring defrosts the body in the creek." It sounds awkward. Like a translation.

Kill the translator.

*

Save "modernism."

Kill.

Burn through the media.

I don't break apart, I break together.

The river is not the river of water, it's the bombing.

*

Dream: I was shown two corpses to identify. One represented Culture and the other was obviously female. I chose Culture to operate on. I found the exit wound and the entry wound just where I suspected they would be. It had happened several times. It was not a drive-by shooting or the work of a maniac. And there was poison in the blood. Silver poison. The body weighed twice as much as an average corpse. It must have been left in the water for days. Its features had become distorted. I identified it based on the image of the grail tattooed on its belly. I put on eyeliner before examining the next body. The starlet's body had also been drowned; and it too had entries and exits perforating the smooth exterior. I concluded: It was the same killer.

*

Only the shovel works on my body.

*

In this, I am merely doing what the abortion protesters had suspected me of long ago: arson, lullabies, lubbalies, sound collages. I am getting wormy for the final showdown with the Sensation.

I am sensational with my theater cunt and my bruises and my bang-bang-ugh.

Ugh.

Dans Muzique.

I have a corset made for the party, the text.

For "modernism."

*

According to the official narrative of the tabloids and eyewitness accounts, the Starlet refused to come out of her trailer, refused to continue her life as a Starlet because she felt assaulted and molested by fame, she felt uncomfortable with the sexualizing of her innocence. But that's not why she refused. In her mansion with doves nailed to the wall, we conducted a far more intricate savagery. Although I am nervous and twitchy and though I have two holes in my back, I came out alive. I came up for air. I breathed. I am alive but I don't tell this story to the expresident. I tell him about her outfits: the red one with animals taped to the edge, which trailed on the floor, and bashed the animals' skulls against the marble; the skirt she made me wear to the atrocity kitsch; the cap she placed on her blue hair when she video-taped a muzzled girl imitate a muzzled girl with agent orange on her skin (it was the skin dance, it was the orange dance, it was a war dance; it was never successful). Mostly what she was interested in was History.

*

Faster and faster

for a long time you wouldn't feel anything

then you would burst into fire

I didn't know all the places I would go and still one of the most wonderful things is that you get to the set and the layers you go so much deeper than you thought you were going to go.

*

"Puce Moment"

*

The criminal photographer's camera shot is like the fashion lens. The walls are purple in here. Everyone is bruised more or less. I'm almost strangled.

There's a female picture of my childhood. It's prosthetic in the sense that none of those arms are mine and I'm just beginning to get rid of the cosmetics. The choreography is perfect. Perfectly like arrival.

*

Everyday there are supposed photographs of the Black Man on the news and in the newspapers. Most are immediately dismissed as fraudulent. There are only a few certified photographs of him and they keep getting reproduced in various settings every day. Of course some of the fraudulent photographs are also recreated in new settings. And the weird thing is, the more frequently they are reproduced, the more authentic they seem. It's almost as if the Black Man has to be dead already. Only as contamination could he proliferate like this. My favorite photograph in this genre is "Death Grin", where he appears in a collage of horses, naked bodies and a blood-soaked courtroom. No, my favorite is "The Black Man is Alone in the Black Woods." It looks like someone spilled ink on it. It should never have been published.

*

New Jerusalem was not built in a day read the poster affixed to the door and I have a nail in my head, a black girl's black fingernail. That's how I have my cysts removed for the final showdown in which I will inevitably dissect Father Voice-Over and use his internal organ to make the kind of camera that can capture Beauty the way gay porn from the 80s can capture the elegance of abortionists and ghost-sonateers. I will get that close to brilliance.

*

We have to keep the virgins breathing.

*

This novel is written for breathing virgins. To help them understand the wonder that is their skin to help them perform admirably. To teach them about heroic and half-shot-out buildings. To hurt them so correctly they will never doubt that they have been hurt in the kill. This is a novel about the black-and-white virginity of early cinema, the body tricked into doubles and contortions. Hello I am you.

*

Hello. I don't know if I can even take my erotics that far without ruining the projection booth.

*

Hello. Today our topic is female authorship.

All the girls in the audience groan.

Are they having an orgasm?

No they've seen this dress-up-dummy show and they hated it the first time they hated it with scissors and awls and my chest and hypnosis.

You are aroused with scorpions said Father Voice-Over but nobody believed him. Not this time. Not this time. That's what the women kept saying as I shoved the thumbtacks in. Not this time.

Not this time.

*

Most people are suspicious of photographers because they fear catching the reproductive relationship to reality. It seduces, this constant image-proliferation. I must be bad. Ever since I was brought to this goo-goo nation, I've trafficked in images. About photography, I love the machinery. I can't understand any of it. It's like the inside of a woman's cunt: fascinating and intricate. And it gives birth to millions of childrenchildren, sturbations, soundproof sloppy bodies, revolvers. I was a photographer before I was a silk-boy. I was a photograph before I had death in my cock, in my mouth, on my chin. Before my dress caught fire. Before my arms crinkled. The stage crashed. The audience cried. I was photography before I was arson. Before I entered Sister Dark with my scum-cock full of rabies. Before I was a photograph I was a child of art.

*

The rifle doesn't work!

The silver paint is peeling!

You can see my face. It was made for hares.

I wear a corset for the sensation.

Knock. Knock.

I have rehearsed my kissing disease with ground meat.

Perhaps there will be additional make-up.

If my baby is pregnant it will tarnish my image. Her body is colored in. She's in the cake. She has a black body. I have a silver bullet.

Seizure.

The doctor must leave. He has accidentally left the Japanese item on the bleeders' bodies.

Horse death of transcendence: we're in American after all.

*

ratted out

Softcore spiritualism

cinematic bodies

cold

clumsy revulsion

Continue to play on your toy piano

arms that glow in the dark

I love opium

Why are you looking at me like that, little horro. You need to get out of here!

Get out!

I have a nightmare about hair. I'm a child. I fall into a hidden well in a field around where I grew up. I wake up soaked in sweat, my wife stroking my hair. When I tell her about the dream, she tells me what horse carcasses has to do with hair, with videos, with the swarm sounds that erupt in an empty well, as empty as a hole in the head. She says the horse appears to be powerful but there is something vulnerable about its powerful body. "It is always on the verge of getting slaughtered or surrounded by the swarm of copies, which is Art," she explains. Thus my vision of the prairie littered with horse carcasses covered with flies, spears sticking out of them. "But why do I always dream of these massacred horses?" My wife walks over to the window. The anti-abortion protesters are playing war with shopping carts and cancer patients. "All of this was started by your daughters," she says gravely. I don't have a son, I don't have a son.

*

I love faces. I love faces covered with snow. I love the Black Man's many faces. I love the faces I see when I close my eyes. But most of all I love my wife's face, which looks like Frida Kahlo's face. It's dangerous to touch.

*

It seems like everybody around here would be more pleased if I were a moron. As it stands, my detailed knowledge of contorted anatomies and the means by which I have learned how to dress such intricate anatomies makes many of the other inmates jealous, makes the protesters feel implicated in my symptoms. My symptoms include the shakes and a form of verbal disorientation I like to call "Fuck Mouth." They want to wound my fuck mouth. All of them. Fill it up with fois gras.

*

Puke

*

My shangri-la politics are based on ecstatic anorexia.
My demeanor is based on my mash-ups of various hit songs.

*

It's unclear what the Black Man looks like. Judging from most drawings he has a large body which moves flamboyantly. But in one series of images he's very skinny and seem to move like a puppet or automaton. In one he's even playing the piano and grinning at the audience. In most images he's glazed with sweat. In my favorite version he's impersonating Abraham Lincoln.

*

Dear Black Man,

As a Father I am modeled on a dead martyr. As a thief I am re-dundant like a virgin and look for a way out. In the mirror I look sloppy on the rocking horse. I pick the splinters out of my daughter's hair. She's been playing Father again with the dead girls. She can't understand me when I'm out of character. That's when I speak a black, private language, a language for screaming in.

As a Starlet I have a yellowish skin. The magic lantern shakes and quakes. As a Starlet I wear a blouse bunched beneath my armpits and a brand of eyeshadow produced from the glittering skin of fishes. They keep such fishes in wells.

*

This is High Culture and fever starvation immolation rituals.

Lust murders cannot be taken out of context. They are part of a prevalent aesthetic. I am part of a convulsionography I cannot abandon.

Something is fishy about the way I move and scream.

Ignore the subtitles.

*

The soldiers are getting increasingly both horrified and excited about news of the Black Man. They scream an anthem: "Death is a Black Man with his Snakes out!" I don't understand the chants, but Father Voice-Over seems to like it. He chants along over the PA system: "Hang him from a tree with cinnamon!" Some of the soldiers are wearing vampire teeth, which leads me to suspect that they have somehow made contact with the anti-abortionists. "Let us out" they shout and pound the door. No way.

*

The Grotesquerie Takes Over with Lamp Lights and Intricates the Bodies: I am increasingly seeing that I am on an adjacent side to the Anti-Abortionists. I am in favor of the rampant state. It glows in my deer-brain.

Art: I want to abuse all of its excremental tricks and shell games. I want to look at a photograph of the starlet through a semi-translucent membrane.

*

The expresident has written a poem about a sunset with a crown of shark's teeth but I am too busy with my new implements to even read it. I eat some caviar with a cocaine spoon. In haute surveillance the wives are always missing. The men have trouble breathing. The rabid girl tell me over the phone that if it weren't for the actors and actresses I would have no museum to sleep in no doctors to provoke no splinters in my thighs no champagne in hiroshima and no snow on the trees outside the broken windows. That's not snow silly.

*

While walking through the polished corridors I wonder why there are always construction workers wandering through the hallways, their faces covered with sawdust, their hands swollen. It must be that the mansion is expanding, that the number of inmates is increasing at a rapid rate. Maybe there are two "smashed virgins" now. I won't know most of the inmates, but they will know me. I'm the poster child for panic disorders.

*

Look! That's me! The one with the heart!

*

It has begun to dawn on my that I'm never going to be rich. I'll never afford that white-whitest spoon with which I've dreamed of eating caviar. As a result all my performances have been staggering exaggerations.

*

There is a Christ-like quality about the Black Man. But instead of having ants crawl in and out of his body, the Black Man moves around incessantly. According to one news source, he's even been spotted at the White House (though the photograph doesn't look like him at all).

*

Father Voice-Over's Secret Guard is noisy, bawdy and wears funny outfits. They dance in Technicolor. They'll pretend to crown you the Prince of Mutilated Fetuses just for kicks and then they'll slit your throat. They'll make instruments out of your innards and whelky organs. The animals will shriek. They're a joyful bunch.

This is what the expresident whispers to me.

They told me I was their prince, he adds somberly.

Then makes a decapitation gesture with his hand across his throat and whistles.

*

I also think I see a photograph of an atomic explosion back, behind the judge with the blood mush in his face. But I'm not sure why someone would sneak that into the recreation.

*

The doctor comes into my room while I sleep and wipes off my insect nerve but leaves the ganglia to be cleaned off by the nurses. Their lips taste like strawberry and chicken carcass.

One nurse has fingers that smell like honey. She thinks I need more silver in my make-up. She asks me if I am finished with my movie script because the elections are coming up and if it doesn't get made soon it might become obsolete. I tell her it has become a play.

The only people who go to the theater these days are people who secretly yearn to be torch-bearers and people who can't go home, she says. A little juice trickles down her chin. Oops! she exclaims and wipes it off with her forearm.

*

If I were wearing a mask at that instance it would be the gas mask of all things bleak. A fondling mask so to speak.

Instead I have to watch a movie about firing lines.

It is a travesty.

*

I am not photogenic in this light.

*

In the shower stall I feel pretty because of the flowers and strings and sparkly things. But they cover up my head for the shoot. I hear a dog but I know it's a recording. I can hear someone press rewind and then play. I know I am naked because I'm cold and posed like a whacked mother, suggesting shame. It's a hilarious concept because I hear people laughing. I would laugh too but my mouth is tied up. I would escape but there are birds on my body and birds are expensive they must not be ruined. I'm hungry because this is a religious occasion. "Corrupt Pope," it's called. The man who says that is also chewing what sounds like a burger.

*

In another fever: My father walks through the room in a nightgown, the trail held up by fever-asian girls. The trails are made of meat. When the girls hold them up for the audience, everyone boos. I'm in the wooden carousel. The Black Man who escaped from his own trial is hiding inside the horse.

*

My father is the mother of this tale because he was the one who took me to America. He wanted his life to be a movie.

*

To an immigrant, the world is a movie. To an American, a foreigner has a video body. Hang me in a tree or a lamppost. Dingle-dangle. I'm a Christmas ornament from the old world.

Everything I touch becomes Art.

*

Marc Jacobs: New York Boston Los Angeles San Francisco Las Vegas Hong Kong Taipei Beijing Shanghai Manilla Doha Jeddah Kuala Lumpur Bal Harbour Honolulu Madrid London Istanbul Kuwait City Athens Milan Dubai Sao Paulo Tokyo Jakarta Moscow Riyadh Paris Beirut Osaka Ho Chi Minh City Seoul Macao Manama Hanoi Shen-zhen

*

One of my youngest daughters is horribly pregnant. We think she accidentally licked a towel that my wife had been using to wipe herself after sex. Thus she received a contaminated sexual material which then developed in her smelly belly. She has given birth to six babies and I fear the worst. I fear more are on the way. This daughter goes by the fancy name The World. But we don't use that name.

*

Outside the hospital the anti-abortionists are performing a piece about exit wounds.

*

The expresident has the swine flu. One of the nurses suggested as much by oinking. Her entire body shuddered and she oinked. She has a tattoo right above her ass. It is smeared. She slapped me because I came all over her back. So far the anti-abortionists's performances have not been realistic enough.

I could tell them about the expresident's flu. I could also tell them where the dead birds used in tests are discarded.

The anti-abortionists have come to the Shining Mansion on the Hill for the same reason I came here: violence, serial production, the imaginary, the voice.

*

Postcards are created from history. Sexuality is a strange fruit hanging from a strange and possibly infected tree.

*

But where does fear come from?

Answer: The Father, mainly. But also from outmoded art and plastic masks (wearing them, not looking at them, unless you are looking at them through a mirror).

*

I see a billboard today that says "An abducted child is everyone's child." One thought I have is how this mania for abducted children obfuscates the much more prevalent crime of fathers molesting their children. I realize that I am the opposite of the abducted child. I have too many daughters.

*

One of my daughters refuses to shit. My wife and I stuff her with fruits and chemicals but she refuses to shit. She shudders holding it in. When she finally shits she screams and cries and her shit is blood-muddled. That's the kind of place this is.

This "America." Virgin land.

*

John Locke treated words as a kind of currency that became valuable only when backed up with a model of interiority. Words are susceptible to inflation. Insects pile up. I write poetry.

*

All these versions of the Black Man – screaming, with a ransom note, tainted on his nails, with a female face, with an ugly face, with a scar – suggests a kind of inflation of his image. He is an icon but an icon that is constantly changing, becoming worthless. Even his original crime has been forgotten. He is now saturated by the atmosphere of criminality.

*

The expresident asks me why my writing is so full of hate and I tell him it's because I'm searching for the enemy.

*

The expresident spends most of his time researching black bodies. He is particularly interested in skin diseases and the bodies of black men who have worked as stunt doubles on particularly violent movies. The expresident is particularly interested in black stunt bodies involved in car crashes. He is a nostalgic man, this expresident we're propping up in the corner.

*

Because I am an anorexic I mostly subsist on wafers. Even when the salt is gone I can taste it there, on my wife's lips.

Because I am anorexic I only eat the cheapest caviar and drink the cheapest champagne.

Mother Machine Gun rebukes me: you are a poet you need to eat your caviar on a spoon made from the bones of small children, you need to drink champagne out of my dirty dirty hand, this hand which I have used to feed arsenic to the president's president.

*

The soldiers are having trouble with the octopus imagery, I'm having trouble with the winding stairs.

When violence is contaminated, there is nothing left to keep love innocent.

The interiority clearance: you can have it for free once it's poetry.

I'm raising a toast tonight to the smashed piano in the corner.

I'm toasting the bodies of teenage girls.

I'm playing the stuffed fox with my lips.

One boy keeps getting obliterated by religious iconography. And in his obliteration, millions of other victims of hate crime are subsumed under religious iconography. (I'm talking about Matthew Shepard of course.)

*

I'm talking about electrical wires.

Sometimes we have to hate.

Sometimes we have to hate, repeats the expresident softly.

Sometimes I look at the strippers and I love their soft bodies that jiggle as they strut around the stage.

In one beautiful room the women move their mouths but they do not make a sound and they appear confused by my sign language.

I make a motion like I am being attacked by snakes.

They make a motion like they wipe off my ganglia with thinner.

*

The strippers think I have an insect body but I have a numb show.

When reading the numb show, you should always keep a reminder of Whitey nearby. It is for him I am drawing a snake in the white cum on my belly.

If you cannot find a white person, you can wear a doctor's white coat. Or you can fashion a crude doll of sorts out of paper towels. Burn it when you're through. You don't want to leave any evidence of the fact that you know what this numb show is about: black bodies, 19th century bodies, burn victims, cinematic natives.

I am more shot in a horse's head than royalty.

More cancer, more black leotards, more cake for the sweethearts, more hard-ons for the voice, more explanations for the melancholiacs.

Sometimes I think that the only way out of here is through starvation.

*

When I was a child I once watched a news report about the Vietnam War. Agent Orange, burning draft cards, torn sheets of deceitful propaganda reports: the sawdust that covers my hair and skin as I walk the corridors of this mansion reminds me of that program. It's the same theory of media.

*

The Soldiers want to perform a new play about the Black Man. I'm sorry, I say, that mis-en-scene looks terrible, like something you might steal from a billionaire who wants to kill all Palestinians. They look deflated. They were hoping I would star as myself, "The Killer," and that I would wrap myself in that flower-splattered winding sheet.

*

In some ways, we're all in here because of contamination. We're Beautiful.

*

The expresident wakes me up whispering: I feel stifled, pallid, mealy-mouthed. What makes this odd is that he's speaking out of his throat-machine. His actual mouth adds: There is a precarious interchange between language and the world. I'm it.

*

The expresident tells me I represent Transcendence, a blatant trope of eluding the voice-over, or of sprawling around for the voice-over, or of killing the voice-over's pale, elaborate and tingly body. I must be a killer. The anti-abortionists cheer in the yard.

They've discovered a new way to hate.

The expresident thinks the Black Man must be trained as an actor. There is no way he could otherwise elude all these police officers and vigilante mobs if he was not professionally trained, he reasons. He thinks the Black Man must be a veteran of the war.

*

All morning the expresident and I play "hide and seek" in the mausoleum, which is full of blankets that have to be disinfected for the inauguration of the new president.

*

This is how I've come to think of the Virgin Father: As an exhibitionist with long, slender legs and a fat belly.

This is how I've come to see Father Voice-Over: Eradicate.

The former's methods include animal experiments and modern architecture. The latter's method is to authenticate.

*

I don't dare to wake you up but I wanted to show you a picture I found in the bed just now: dead horses, dead soldiers.

*

I want to go home to Ho-Chi-Minh City I tell my daughter. There they will appreciate a lover such as myself. They will pay for my oink-oink heart to be examined.

They will pay me with scorpions in the hair.

When I return to the US, I will use subtitles to contradict the voice-over.

I will fuck up the Symbolism of the drowning victim by suggesting that we use some imagery from Mad Cow's Disease. This would make it an allegory, which is not the preferred method.

No the heroine does not die.

That is me slumped over in the corner. I am hungry and maybe strangled. Mostly I am anorexic.

*

One day the soldier's fetal lamb pose looks a little different. It looks more like festering fruit than a fetal lamb. It's from another chapter of the book, explains one soldier while shaving his chest and genitals. Holding the mirror, I'm grateful for that. They should all look like stunted children. That's my work of Art, but they haven't realized it yet. They think I'm here to teach them how to write poetry. The fetal lamb pose apparently is not sincere enough. It's based on a translation. Arsenic imagery. Soft bodies. It's all terrible. I've been told to stop teaching these naked killers, but I never taught them anything. They welcomed me home.

*

The Black Man has already been spotted all over the country, in various disguises. Anybody could be him anywhere at this point. We've noticed an increase in protection at the mansion. They're scared he'll show up in here, says the expresident. As victim or inmate, I ask him. What kind of place do you think this is, says the expresident with outrage. The kind of place where bodies are smeared with fruit, I answer. He'll come here only if he belongs here, says the expresident. Judging from the television he belongs here.

*

Twinkle music for pony slaughters

Or: twinkle slaughters for pony music.

Girls with freedom's medallion pinned to their chests

*

I've become evil because language gets in the way.

*

The fire alarm in the ceiling includes a small vial of bright-red blood. Blood is very sensitive to convulsions.

The elevators seem to be broken or I'm scared of hotels it's where ghosts accumulate.

We're in a hotel-motel-massacre-inn.

*

I hate mirrors because they remind me that I'm a Father who keeps reproducing. Whenever I see a camera, I have the urge to pull it open and pull out all the littery slippery pieces. No more reproduction. The digital camera is frightening. It seems to reproduce without involving any matter. Not even dark matter. I know this is suicide.

*

It's horrible the way I forget that I am a Father and then I remember when I'm applying the white-face paint in the mirror. I see that I'm becoming a Father.

*

Every day on television there are reports of the Black Man committing strange crimes across the country. He hijacked a car and drowned the children, he wore a Mickey Mouse mask, he let a woman go because she was touched by angels, he stole a cape and a hood from a convenient store, he fucked a young man up the ass while telling him his plans for a race war, he used a glass shard to cut another man's chest red, he left drug paraphernalia in a young woman's bedroom (he had a cut on his chest, she said). For every latest news item about the man, the expresident becomes strangely convinced that the man is getting closer to the Mansion. Convinced that he's drawn to me, to my corpse-like physique, to my hairless physique, to my cunt-mouth.

*

It's in my role as Father Make-Up that I wander the hallways searching for Love and Death midst the heaps of dead girls.

*

Myth of Origins: The Starlet was brought in on a platter. She was not born so much as she was hosed off, disinfected. In her first movie, she shuddered in white as history was replayed as a farce. The ghastly chamber she hid in when the killers stalked her in the second movie was where I imagined surviving my teenage years. When she was shiny and happy in the third movie, she looked terrifying to me. I was already a bleeder in the snow. You were already writing your application to college in fuchsia ink. My mouth was sloppy from the meat. My ribcage was rattled from the impact. I passed out at a concert. A thousand arms carried my body through the air. A thousand arms carried me through the shakedown, the fake-out. My body glistened in the video, which was a party of science fiction. I played the son. You played the hostess.

*

(Get out of here! Clear the set!)

*

The soldiers will perform *The Screens* as a way of expressing their feelings about the bombing of Gaza.

Even the excised part celebrating the aesthetics of the failed abortion.

I tell the expresident that I love pig meat.

He tells me, Most people will convince you never to engage in kinomutilations.

Father Voice-Over asks that we use rat-poison to solidify our roles in haute surveillance.

*

Dear dead girl,

You would not be nearly so poetic if I weren't already so frozen, if I hadn't already shot a hare that made the winter red.

*

The expresident thinks I'm here because I have eating problems. He thinks, given the right circumstances, I would eat human flesh.

My wife laughs. She has had a repeated vision of me eating our children.

You're both involved in a culture of death. You're abortionists and abolitionists! cries the expresident, full of moral outrage.

His face is blue from the light outside the window.

*

Atrocity Kitsch #2: Soldiers are putting on a production based on Arabian Nights. I am trying out for the part of the massacred wife as a way of understanding the war. When I get on stage the soldiers tell me to put a hood on. Stand still, they keep saying. This won't hurt, they keep saying. Quiet, they keep screaming. I am as quiet as a massacred wife. I can hear their cameras. I'm freezing. I think I can go now. I can't.

*

Moral: Actors make the best soldiers. They will kill like it's an act. It's an act. They will find me in the swimming pool. They'll pretend to stab me repeatedly in the chest.

*

The expresident thinks the Black Man is coming to the mansion in order to assassinate me. He's not sure why but he thinks it has to do with the starlet and the underground movies we made together before her death. Didn't you have a movie about a black man prostrate on the floor, ink running out of or into his body? No, I reply, that was me in black face and it was supposed to be blood. That movie was a colossal failure. Even the Starlet hated it and wanted to burn it and hang its plastic corpse from a tree branch.

*

This part of the novel takes place in black face, which means you should imagine us all as white. Covered in cocaine. In snow. In white skin from an animal so white it is an unanimal. A plague. In this episode, Ladies and Gentlemen, we pull the scorpions out of our bobs. It's Baghdad. Protect the scalpels when the looters come. Prepare to see the world through gasoline fumes. Walk on stilts.

Confession: I was januaried in my eyes. I abused my ganglia, misused it as a hook of sorts. It was the thing to do at news conferences.

I need a breather.

The expresident needs the silencer.
I've stolen it.
I'm ready for a New Beginning!

The expresident's fantasies of the Black Man:

1. The Black Man is "a national tragedy."
2. The Black Man's torso modeled on swinery and deceit.
3. The Black Man is a star, posing in front of photographers with a swan and a bundle of money that is burning.
4. The Black Man as an emperor of sorts – the kind poisoned, naked, covered with shards.
5. The Black Man has come to eliminate all White People, and thus to save us from ourselves.
6. Beautiful white china plates.
7. A horrible allegory acted out under duress of military officers with bags over our heads.
8. A hole in our cultural fabric, a leak in the language of progress.
9. As asexual
10. As inhuman
11. As an allegory about death.
12. That he's a woman.
13. That he's meaningless.

The acousmatics of my room are creepy. I wake up from small children yelling. When I wake up, Father Voice-Over informs me that the rabbits are dying painfully. I must record my voice so that I can play it back slowly. I may be able to find a clue to a hidden crime, somewhere in there, in the collapse.

In part because the body signifies a proverbial replacement.

In other words, I give you my childhood, you give me an odalisque with money in her snatch. I give you comfort from the scandalous world of fashion, you idealize me, placing a rose behind my ear.

It's a deal for the radiantly impoverished.

*

Sometimes I want a room of my own, but mostly I just want a room without all this corpse-patterned wallpaper. This mansion is said to have been built by the same man who built the war, but I think it was his brother, who unfortunately had the same white teeth, the same love of the PA system. No doubt the corpses were modeled on the war, or the other way around. Sometimes Art drips. Other times I imagine a tiger-mauling of a man in velvet, or a woman drowning in the bathtub. In that scene, the Art is in her hair, which pours out of the tub and down on the wet floor.

Art mostly is about nostalgia.

*

Tithe-Hole: In the wards for cleaning holes, the paint is chipping off the walls. It reminds me of Berlin when I was a child and Berlin here stands in for an abortion clinic. It was during the cold war, I explain.

The nurse can't answer because she has something in her mouth and anyway she doesn't speak English and I'm covering up her mouth.

My entire body is gleaming with turpentine!

She's done!

I'm unrecognizable with the bandages, but the crown, the crown really gives me away.

*

The expresident thinks the Black Man is out to get me because I act like a moron.

*

The PA system goes spastic, screams tearing through the entire mansion. Sounds like a technical malfunction but the expresident says it's a black woman screaming. Don't take away my baby, she says according to the expresident. No, she says, Don't sell me, according to my wife. The anti-abortionists seem to agree with the expresident's interpretation. They are preparing something that looks like sloppy blankets, handling them with plastic gloves. To me it sounds like a voice without meaning, or a commodity screaming out its own matter, its own dark matter. It's a voice that will have a million children and they will all die. Their executioners will wear plastic gloves. Their spectators will wear barely anything at all on their damaged, television-horny bodies.

*

I am moving on to the classroom where I learned to count victims.

An orphan drowns in the ice. A national myth.

I am skinny and damaged and about to faint.

The Black Man is reproducing his trial with perverse silhouettes.

One silhouette is of the judge with a hole in his head.

Another is a silhouette of the Starlet with her cunt and her swimming pool.

The most ridiculous silhouette tells me that I'm not alone. It looks like a fetus but it's symbolic. It's Love. It's Slaughter. It's nailed to the walls of the court room.

The most beautiful silhouette seems dragged out of a sack and glued together.

The most fragile silhouette has already been ruined. Soiled. The Black Man must have jacked off on it. It's the silhouette that represents dark matter. It's got a day-of-the-dead look, all bony and protruding. A myth about the body-in-media.

The expresident thinks he knows everything about the Black Man even though it's all based on fables and conjectures.

The Black Man has a visionary body, according to the ex-president. The kind of body that blurs the boundaries between spirituality and hate crimes.

The Black Man's body may, according to the expresident, be modeled on historical documents. It may be smeared. It may be so dark that it cannot be seen except in recreations. It may be sexual in a dysfunctional way. Like fucking in the same bathtub where you drowned your children.

*

Lets go back to the Starlet because she was indeed murdered. This is afterall a story about her voice. Lets consider her vision of the wound. She saw it as a feature of language. For example, when I tried to explain to her why pussy wasn't the right translation, she turned on the radio. She pointed to the horse skeleton on her wall. She plugged an earring in my ear. It was a green stone. Blood trickled down my earlobe. She shot me and shot me. Do you want to know how I posed? I posed with a disgusting clarity in my eyes for I saw myself as a Subject of a Very Important Feature on Body Doubles. If you were to see those pristine photographs today you would doubt that the Starlet had taken them. You would not believe they could be taken by the same woman who made all those muffled movies, all those torn photographs, all those staged assassination attempts, all those painful masks and ornaments that looked like savagery. You would think these photographs were taken by a riding instructor in love with extermination.

*

My new wound is stapled shut with metal staples to keep the blood from leaking out of me.

In B-movies the human body becomes more beautiful and less a subject.

A stunt double.

Ronald Reagan brought me to this country – me and the anti-abortion movement.

The unanimals.

*

Now look at the anti-abortionists: their iconophilia has overwhelmed their country. Just today I saw a truck on campus covered with supposed fetus-limbs, doll-arms hanging from the bumper sticker, scrappling against the pavement.

*

The Starlet was more beautiful inside ambulances than anywhere else.

*

Can't you tell from this lyrical poem that I'm still clambering around in the mansion, trying to find my way out?

*

Everyone's a spy. I've read the files.

Even bicyclists and joggers in the background.

Reagan is dead but I'm still spazzing around in front of this mirror trying to perform an unborn dance.

I'm still bleeding from the head. Still exhausted and luridly posed next to a time bomb.

In all my films the women are hairless.

Death drive.

My wife is in the cutting room trying to make sense of these contradictory images. She is preparing for the catwalk. To help her I have brought her various reels of footage. It will give me nightmares.

*

My wife is already planning the decoration of my ganglia and my insect nerve and my black face.

My wife is watching Cocteau's remake of *Helter Skelter*. She's onto something. She senses in me the inexcusable urge for ridiculous race wars.

When I get to the bottom I keep looking at an image from another film. The woman is naked except for black underwear.

I might find her in the underground. I need to pull the panties down so that I can see what flower she has placed in her snatch. There is a massacre going on outside. The bomb light is ruining the film.

*

One student tells me he found my PA announcements about the Gaza Strip "very moving."

The expresident told me: You weren't there, you didn't see anything.

He was speaking on film.

*

The Genius Child Orchestra's video is on video. Their colors blear. They have no future. Because they have no place. They have prostheses, not community. They have a neck made for necking. And their visuals are parasitic.

*

The Soldiers think I'm playing the Genius Child Orchestra's latest video in order to mock them. It's called "Be Who You Are," and it's about death. Why do you have to mock us, they ask me. They make war seem like an act of decorating horse carcasses with flowers. They make war seem like a mirror that has been stained. They make war seem like pregnant women. They make war seem like snowy bodies. They make war seem almost fun. Don't you think war is fun? I ask them. Yes it's fun but at the same time it's scary and horrifying. I once drove into a girl who was picking up a water bottle from the road, can you contact her? One of the soldiers asks me. I can't, I say, but they can, I say, and point to the Genius Child Orchestra now visible in the dim light of the television, they can contact her with their hot bodies.

*

Later I found out that a doctor had doctored the footage of a burned child. I found it very moving. I praise virgins because I imagine that they are my kidnappers.

*

Were I to build a shrine
to my own virginity
I would build it out
of fish skeletons.

It is getting harder for me to tell who is speaking over the PA system or if it is even coming from the PA system or my archaic tapeplayer or if I'm remembering something the Starlet once told me in one of her movies about cocaine. We were naked and moving slowly through a black garden.

*

I eat blackberries. I call them lynching berries. I call them the fruit of genius. Skin berries.

*

Black Dolls: It is no wonder that people became so obsessed with dolls in the 1910s and 20s, fearing that they would take over the world and replace human beings. The reason for this is not so much dolls and mannequins but seeing human bodies in the movies. It is no wonder that the doll-craze returned in the late 1960s and early 70s when we were watching bodies getting blown up and burned to crisp on the nightly news. This trend will continue and the War in Iraq will soon lead to paranoia about dolls.

But this time it will be about the dolls we cannot see.

Screwy dolls that taste like licorice.

*

But someone else will have to smear the dolls in creams. My hands are virginal. Anti-hands.

That has to do with Art, not the snatches of teenage girls. Notice how white my spoons are. They are the spoons of homosexuals. They are public spoons made for force-feeding prisoners. They are the sex spoons of terrorists. They are the fox spoons of Nature. They are cocaine-blessed.

*

The Aesthetics of Embarrassment: The plague itself, even when it's called "Hurricane Katrina," must be given its proper due. Modern cinema is born out of infested water and starvation. We must not leave this image. This is where we create a loot cinema about "the anti-abortion movement."

*

You have never watched the birds like I watch them.

On the children's television.

Like I have the plague like little girls have the plague.

Everywhere in this movie the little girls are dying.

It might be a literary reference or an alternative to the Oedipal complex. It might be JonBenét Ramsey Complex. All these staged and mutilated bodies that have to be hauled onto the screen over and over.

The moral has to do with beauty. A kind of beauty that is hidden in basements or suitcases. A hare-like beauty.

Perhaps it's an aesthetics, not an ethics.

*

My daughter and I practice a metaphysical regime that involves jacklighting. We haul the carcasses back to the capital. Pile them up on the steps of the white house. Get deported. Do it again. It's an exercise in lineage. A gothic childhood: we run away with the devil because we don't want to be married. Get a job, say the soldiers. Get a job, says the PA System. But none of them have jobs. Together we have ruined the zigzag site of the American Gothic. Our animatronic animals suggests we're still in nature. Still Edenic with our black-tipped bodies and cutting disorders.

JonBenét Ramsey Complex: How the reports found her tarted up costumes visually equal to rape and murder. The crime of pageantry. I found Miss World demented and naked in a back-street in the Midwest. The opposite of pageantry. Pageantry.

*

News of the escaped black man has even reached the children's shows. I find the imagery in cartoons particularly graphic.

It's similar to the JonBenét Ramsey Complex, with this difference: he's the perpetrator and we are the victims. But it's the same concept of pageantry as violence. Aesthetics as crime.

*

It's hard to make a corset out of a hare, but I use heroin. I pound and pound with my hammer of gold. A yellow liquid is secreted from my shells. My face looks secret when it appears on anti-abortion posters. It looks joyful in the mirror. The abortion mirror.

The anti-abortionists keep killing doctors who perform abortions: The culture of knock-knock-who's-there?

Answer: The Oedipus Complex.

*

It's hard to explain why film-makers fall back on the Oedipus Myth now that the King is dead once and for all and his daughter won't stop shivering.

It's hard to explain the nacreous mother.

There are laws about such mothers. Disgusting laws in which I play the devil.

*

Boo!

*

When I try to remember my childhood I think of Ronald Reagan, carrying me in a parade of anti-abortionists to the Shining Mansion on the Hill. I'm wearing a hare mask already. The president is explaining pictures to me from a hospital window, which I want to break just to hear the sound he makes.

*

There must be some way to wrest violence away from the newscasters and economists.

*

Why did the Starlet leave the limelight so hastily? Everybody asked her and she never answered. But several times she told me, as we were working on our last film, the story of a photoshoot in which she appeared painted in silver. As the photographer's assistants applied the paint, they reassured her that it wasn't chemical, that it wouldn't hurt her, that it would be easy to remove. "It felt so cold on my skin," she kept repeating to me as she covered me in torn strips of silk. When they had finished with the shoot, however, she couldn't get the paint off. At first she used water, but it just smeared the paint. She started using soap but none of it worked. Increasingly frantic, she started scrubbing herself with a brush that scarred her skin and made her bleed. Finally an assistant saved her by dousing her with thinner that made her scratched skin burn and burn. It was traumatic, she told me. But she did not tell me why she chose to recreate it with me in the role of the beloved. She wanted to reproduce it because she was fascinated by the liquids.

*

The expresident is conflicted about modernism. He fears he betrayed not just his wife by moving into this Shining Mansion, but also the ideals of modernism – its heroic opposition to kitsch and mass culture, its ideal of form=function, its privileging of architectural metaphors. He fears that indeed this is why he's been brought to this mansion, this grotesque site where everything proliferates. I ask him if he thinks his wife believes in modernism. No, he says and puts on his breathing mask. His breathing mask is decorated with golden studs. If you look very closely, you will see that on each stud there is a tiny skeleton engraved.

*

When the expresident describes the Black Man, all the bodies seem to leak. In fact, any time the expresident discusses bodies, he generates a vision of America as a country covered in fluids. The expresident has begun to collect postcards of lynchings. He says they remind him of his lover. His lover had scars which got irritated when they were in the woods. His lover wrote a letter to his own wound. Dear Wound, the letter began, they are looking for us all over the place – you, me and the president – but they will never find us, not as long as stay disguised in the woods and shoot guns at the pound-dolls.

*

The expresident doesn't believe I understand the nature of trauma. It happens once, then it affects you secretly ever after, he explains. But I refuse. The trauma saturates the mansion, it's a trauma-rama. I have a brooch that has been handed down through generation even though it was a piece of crap. My grandfather gave it to my grandmother after he got her pregnant at a fascist youth rally. It's a beetle on two leaves, coated with dull gold glitter.

*

I do not want my body to be hung up for show.

*

The Virgin Father wore a nightgown as he carried me through the melee. This will not save him and it won't protect me from vultures.

*

My nude body is not fit to be interviewed. My holes have been corrupted and there is snow on my copy of Dreyer's *Joan of Arc*. I want to compare the erotics of that movie with the erotics of idiots like me, people who sleep in ding-dong dormitories.

I will polish up my make up.

"That's better," says the expresident. "Now I can tell that you've been traumatized by experience."

I've been traumatized by Art. Ridiculed by Experience.

*

According to the news reports, the Black Man is either capable of miraculously moving through the most plague-ravaged parts of the country without getting sick, or he's already suffering from numerous diseases. A young woman who claims she was temporarily kidnapped by the Black Man says he coughed and was "all shuddery," suggesting to one reporter that he's indeed dying. However, another reporter believed this was evidence that the girl was lying. The expresident looks at her image and says, "That girl, I've seen that girl before. I think she's a prostitute in town. He is getting close."

*

Today I begin with my exaggeration therapy. The first step is to declare that I have a problem with fire arms. The second step is to kiss with my porcelain lips. To kiss money. Goodbye.

The doctors hold the key to the theater state.

Secretion State

Exhaustion State

Lack State

The state I am in would best be described by someone wearing smudged makeup to the train station. I will sell mannequins in the morning. Tomorrow morning I take my daughter to children's music class.

False witness

There can be no immigrants in utopia.

I learned to write because I was poor at stealing. I stole stale meat because I thought it was a notebook. You are here, it read.

Arsenic for nightingales

I'm not taking dictation. This shit is all from me.

Me and my horrible mouth.

I have the shitty eyes of a masturbator. I don't know how to use a comb or a drill. What hope do I have of ever gaining meaningful employment in this rotting mansion.

Note to self: Keep the inflation down.

*

It is so hard to tell if the PA system is functioning and where the noise is coming from. I think it's coming from the anti-abortionists. They leave notes for me in which they claim I owe them something. I owe them and I owe it to Reagan to rub his mask when I fuck my wife.

*

Again the screeching PA system.

The expresident think it's a sign that the Black Man is close.

I think it's the inflation of commodities ruining Father Voice-Over's delicate song.

*

I follow the Black Man's adventures very attentively. They remind me of my own dismemberment exercises and exhaustions. We are both decoys and our entire bodies have been traced with box-cutters.

My camera is sloppy and I am a flabby abortionist and I look bombed-out with this ki-ko-pee body. It's a body that needs and collapses. A virgin crawl. It has a reputation for rashes spazz in ashes. I don't even know how the sperm will function now that my wife is black and black, Spanish, Washed-Up and Given Succor.

*

The expresident wants to know the truth about the Starlet. What did her lips taste like? He suggests strawberry. I can't remember. All my memories are visual. Or else contaminated by my interrogations.

I pose with a rifle.

*

We have to hate teenagers. They are despicable.

We have to love teenagers. Their drugs are beyond reproach.

Passivity is the greatest sin. Fuck me.

When I watch vampire movies I just want the heroes to give up. It may have something to do with the women in the slim orientalist outfits. Or the slaughter that isn't shown on the news.

Actors make the best utopians. They have no problems with the killing act.

*

When I was in high school they put me in the problem student group. That's where I got into drugs. One problem child was a dealer and he suggested new students to be added to the group.

In the latest movie about race war, the black characters act without motivation. That is why they should win. But actors do their finest work while children are being burned alive. Look at them sipping champagne. I love champagne. Why can't I have some of that champagne. Why am I stuck in this looted store with frozen hands. I can't even put the key in the lock, it's so cold.

*

The Starlet liked cut-out paper dolls, especially when I used a knife to cut the dolls out because that would make for a rough look that she felt fit perfectly into our famine parties and she loved to arrange them in peculiar patterns on the floor and sometimes she would tape them on my body. This is why she shaved my body – so that the tape would work, not to infantilize me, as some have suggested in the tabloids. There was a boy she liked to infantilize – for example by shaving him off and then wrapping his penis and testicles in tape – but he was not me. He had a scar across his chest that she also loved. We did a lot with that scar, mostly tenderly. Though once we used gasoline and the utter waste of that operation seems to have upset the boy. I found him crying in the white room. It's the piece we later called "Riding With Death." I'm not sure if it was the camera that was the death of the boy, his skin so dark against the white walls, his crown dripped down his face and chest.

*

Don't touch me I'm sensitive!

*

I have the swine-flu. Transcendence disorder. The voice-over says the doctors are merely replaying the disturbing news with my body but I think they are working towards a new beginning. They feed me the most delicious pink cake.

Tonight they're showing 2001: A Space Odyssey.

The Problem of the Confidence Man: He is the one with the personality. I just have a trance or an operation.

The Curious Nature of Semen: I'm beginning to think the videotape has been damaged.

The Curious Nature of Semen: I am learning how to make use of the numbness in order to fully realize the potential of the numb show. I make the sound of rabbits being born.

And then there are the shell-like bodies which, like my own clammy virgin body, must be hosed off.

*

The hardest truth to swallow is that there are not enough patients.

*

You were in the house, on your knees, in a state of wild terror. You were not a baby anymore. You were not a baby anymore. You were not even human.

*

The Starlet must not have been solemn. She was never solemn, even when she was inserting needles in my skin, even with she was watching my every move with her brilliant god-camera that leaked oil. Even when she was supposedly recording the sound of traffic jams for her portrait of my corpse physique, she was never quite doing so, always twitching, always talking about trauma-ramas, always referring to our production of *The Duchess of Malfi* in a shooting range as the origin of our relationship. She shot me. She shot me hard. She placed flowers in the orifices and spoke into them. When we were finished the whole shooting range stank of powder, resin, semen, arsenic. That is when I realized I was carrying something like death inside my cock.

*

The expresident is certain that I am drawing the Black Man to our mansion, that the Black Man can sense me, that perhaps he's working with the nurses, that perhaps he is already within the mansion walls. He is drawn to me because we are the same kind of homeless, the same kind of criminal. The expresident seems nervous for the first time since he was carried into this room. Even the doctors seem to believe the Black Man is heading for our mansion.

*

When I recreated the starlet with a mute woman she cried in a spasmodic manner, jerking back and forth. My shoes got dirty. My hair was full of muck. I walked around with her snot dried on my throat for days afterwards. It was a failure. She refused to be Pre-Raphaelite. I refused to be embalmed.

The Starlet is the embodiment of American culture. She has blood on her hands. It smears when she gets excited. I should call the abortionists into my room and have them recreate her.

The Starlet was more violent than violated.

*

How does one describe a stunt body? One does not use narrative. To do so would be to ruin the effect of bodies piled up pell-mell and made of silk. One could describe the stunt bodies as stunted and that would make sense if by stunted one meant a physical act that keeps happening. It keeps happening, I tell my wife. Stunt bodies. Stunt bodies. One best describes such bodies on stage using violent means. One might run down the hall to the "corrupt flower" and scream out the descriptions. One could say about stunted bodies that they belong to war, or they are obscene like certain flowers, but one cannot quite write a narrative about them. Sell out. OK, I say to my mirror.

*

In the music hall I try to counteract the poison with a dance, a famous war dance.

*

If the Black Man indeed appears in my room, I imagine we could perform a production of "The Assassination of Abraham Lincoln," in which I could be John Wilkes Booth in beautiful jeans and a sailor's shirt, and he could be Lincoln, naked on the floor, covered in orchids and other fetal imagery. Perhaps he will be surrounded by nuns. Perhaps he will, with the last drops of energy, hold up a hand mirror to his own face to see his true wound.

*

The War Dance is a B-Movie Trope: The whole time I hear voices say "Faster! Faster! Faster!" But I can't go any faster. I can't go any faster.

*

As far as I'm concerned, you no longer belong in the Seraphim Theater. There can be no Starlets in the Seraphim Theater (especially when dead). There can only be soldiers and opera bodies. And the snow is beautiful when it coagulates on the numb-numb in the numb number that follows zero.

If it wasn't for the theater, there would be no cancer, no snow on my skin, no car crash on the highway, no clattering branches, no mass rally, no voice-over attempting to shout out my own voice. When I try to say "It's over," the voice says "It's opera." I'm thrilled. I don't want it to be over.

Maybe I should try to wake up? Maybe I should remove the plastic bag from my head? Maybe I should sing a lullaby for the slippery parts of my body to lull them? Maybe I should use shrapnel for new purposes?

*

The voice-over: "I'm a baby. I have been vomiting up torn toys all night. Can you clever fellows help me score some botox?"

*

There is a hunger strike over at the light-on mausoleum and I'm going to win!

*

The expresident opens up the paper for me. Two pictures: one of a half-naked black man and one of me, pale and glazed with a thin layer of a translucent liquid. The paper speculates if the two most notorious sexual criminals in the country had come to unwholesome ends before being brought before the law. The Starlet took the picture of me with her fake camera. She glazed me over with that semen-like liquid that also tingled like sperm. She loved to depict me as a corpse. She loved the look of semen, loved to play with its death-like properties.

*

She also loved to shave my body, particularly my genitals because she wanted to portray me as a dead child.

*

News organizations are setting up temporary stations in the mansion. When do you expect the Black Man to show up, one reported asks me. I'm wearing a new suit, which was made in China, by a Chinese child listening to a mechanical bird tell them about Art.

*

The cutting room is full of soldiers masturbating. The photographs of me are totally white-white. My wife tells me this as she slathers my pale anorexic body and sings a song about "Europe." It's a song about invasions and trains and wrecks and coups. My favorite part is about the plague.

My second favorite is about hostages.

They are still alive.

I am ready.

For the exhibition.

Today a very loud soldier has invented a new approach to the theater she doesn't even bother to make words, she just gestures wildly and tries to kill me with her nails and then she lets the voice-over say whatever it pleases it says "no no no." I'm not sure if that is what I am supposed to be saying or what she is saying. The sound is not synchronized. I think I should be saying: "We found your child in the rubble." Or: "I wish I could eat your cancer when you turn black." Or: "This lipstick goes great with your disease." I'm really saying: "Leave this place now. The actors are coming to get you!"

*

The expresident has come to an important conclusion: He thinks the only way to protect the inhabitants of the mansion against the escaped Black Man is to take out Father Voice-Over. Here we sit around all day long believing we have a sweet, ethical interior. Meanwhile that Black Man is stalking through our doors and windows. He will get here any day now.

*

It's true what Adorno says: We rent this room. But look at me! What is this but a body built for renting? The rentier's splattered body.

But if I didn't have this room, the Black Man wouldn't know where to find me, kill me. If I didn't have this mirror, he wouldn't know how to do it. I might have to become homeless to survive.

*

The expresident insists that I kill Father Voice-Over to protect the other patients against the horrible threat of the Black Man on the loose. If you don't do it, he explains, the Black Man will find you. By you he means me. He thinks the Black Man is drawn to me. He has sources. Knows inside information. Thinks the Black Man is close to, if not already inside, our Shining Mansion.

*

Don't leave me alone, I tell my wife and grab her arm. I'm not leaving you, I'm just starting to do my work on you. The cork is so hot at first that it burns my skin but after a few seconds it cools off and it feels wonderful to have her stroke up and down my face, my chest, my thighs. I fall asleep in her arms as she goes to work on my silhouette.

*

One TV reporter asks me if I think the Black Man is coming to avenge my alleged murder of the Starlet. I'm sure he doesn't even know who I am, I lie. Then why has he been sending me photographs of himself assuming your poses from the Starlet's movies. Can I see them, I ask incredulously. No, I've burned them because I feared he might use them to track me down, the reporter replies. But if you don't want him to find you, why have you come here? I came here out of my own free will, and that's different.

*

Soldiers have been spotted walking around the corridors of the mansion wearing white gowns and vampire teeth and carrying sticks and stones. The expresident says they're being used to guard against the Black Man. This morning I found a fetal lamb in front of our door. It seemed like a message, but I'm not sure what it says or if it was meant for me or the Black Man. It might be a threat. Or it might mean: this is the door.

*

The expresident loves his paraphernalia – his obscene machine in particular but also his snuff-out flicks and his deck of cards. His favorite card is the hare-king but he won't even let me see it, much less fondle it. "When you've gotten rid of that terrible PA-voice, I'll give you the hare-king to play with in the dark," he says. "It will be your reward. Nobody does anything without an incentive," he says. In the meantime he gives me two cards: the mutilated woman and the burning orphanage. "That's your future," he explains. "That's your past," he explains. Every time he tells his own future he claims he gets the hare-king and the phenomenal vision. That's what he claims but I've never seen it with my own naked eyes. Once I snuck up upon him in the dark and he had a thousand cards and they were all pictures of unconscious bodies in space. Eyes closed. I tapped his shoulder and he twitched. He frantically tried to gather the images into his velvet bag. When he regained his composure he told me "That's just my past." And then: "Use a scissor."

*

The most atrociously beautiful sex is sex on a mirror because the glass breaks and you see a hundred versions of yourself in the shards. This is why the Starlet used mirrors so well in her films. Her films are repulsive with mirrors. It's like the news reports of the Black Man: He is being scattered like mirror shards. He's coming to my room to find the last unbroken mirror of our era: my death mirror. I'll be holding it in the pose of a wounded soldier.

*

The Soldiers and Actors Perform a Dance for the Black Man:

1. Mis-en-Scene: A sunny beach.

2. Audience: American millionaires and their women.

3. Sources: the movies, the photographs, war chants, guides to cutting disorders, pregnancy tests.

4. Movements: They are dynamic with their hand gestures.

5. Props: The horses are cut through.

6. Props: The horses are hung from the walls.

7. Symbolism: The horses are beautiful but criminal.

8. Lesson: The horses suffered in the mansion.

9. Women: played on the horses because the horses were beautiful.

10. Climax: the cameras are cashed.

11. Drugs: cocaine, pot, coffee, speed

12. Poetry: "The Lady of Shalott", "The Palace of Art," "My Last Duchess," "Till Förruttelsen"

13. Media: represented by the flies

14. Media: swarms, rot, retardation

15. Curtains: perfect photographs

The president is moving away from the theory that the Black Man is coming to kill me because of the starlet's death, and toward the idea that the Black Man is coming to kill me because I have no soul. The only way out of the dilemma is still to kill Father Voice-Over.

The wing called "the childish torso" has often been set on fire. I suspect for insurance purposes. The expresident suspects the actors and actresses who have done such a good job teaching me how to imitate a burn victim.

"Mother," I sigh, "a glass of champagne."

*

My lipstick is so shitty, it's hard to see why anybody would want to strangle me.

*

The eyepiece is advertised on the news as a new way of dealing with foreign bodies and also a great place to store your sperm for the French Symbolists, those wonderful lovers of gasoline who drown their pale bodies and cuts and cuts and cuts. They are cinema. They are being transferred to the reliquary.

*

In today's masque, a woman lazily fondled my penis. She applied lipstick to her lips while I applied scars to my black body.

It was a revolutionary moment.

In the next masque all resistance will be tantrums. I will wear the golden bug when I tear apart the ludicrously sharp toys that are shards from the accident.

Then I will improvise an explosive laughter into the megaphone.

*

Our daughter gets pregnant again. This time it's because my wife and I have fucked in the bathtub and forgotten to wash out the tub before giving our daughter a bath. That's what my wife says. I blame photography.

*

The expresident has come up with a new theory for why the Black Man is coming to kill me: he wants to make his image real to us. Apparently the expresident has seen the Black Man walking through the corridors of the mansion, sawdust in his hair and on his face. I have to kill Father Voice-Over soon or it will be all over for us. "The rumors are not true," the PA system announces over and over. A sure sign that the Black Man has arrived.

*

Don't forget to the separate out the trinkets when the soldiers get back. When you leave the Europe room, lock the door. When you are down on your knees with ludicrous things on your mind (hygiene, the shakes, vocabulary lessons), remember that I'm rinsing my hands with thinner because I was told to do so. I believe this has to do with what's coming up next.

*

Today I received an anonymous envelope. Like a message from the beyond, it contained photographs: a smeared X-ray of what seemed to be a bird, a musical stance that was dripping, a torn dress nailed to a wall, a bloodied lip, a shorn hair, a child's coffin decorated with gilded flowers, a penis next to what looks like a busted telegraph, a toy soldier in someone's gloved hand, something anatomical wrapped in a gauze, the mould for a hammer, soiled velvet. These were of course all props from the Starlet's studio, relics from the deeds we filmed there. At first I thought strangely that it was a message from the Black Man, but then I thought it must be someone trying to blackmail me. Blackmail me. I want you to blackmail me.

*

I believe I am supposed to murder Father Voice-Over.

My wife thinks it's an illusion, but the expresident thinks I'm right.

Even before I moved to Hollywood I was an expert in haute surveillance.

*

Before I figured out that there was a voice piped into our room I thought I was haunted by childhood trauma.

*

My wife is talking about the death of bees but she is drawing something in the cum on my belly. The starlet loved bees, but even more she loved the sounds of bee swarms, and would frequently use the sound over just about any image: a beautiful girl in shades, an ambulance carrying a dying hero through the streets, horses piled up on a field, a close-up of a mouth whispering obscenities into the ear of the injured hero. Sometimes when I dream about the Starlet she has bee corpses in her mouth. She spits them out on my body.

*

My wife suggests that I color my face black with burnt cork in order to save me from the Black Man's murderous intent. She says the makeup will draw the man into a space of art where everything is impossible. It will mark the beginning of a new era of the mansion: the era of beauty.

*

The expresident tells me that I'm right about the voice-over. Its role is to arrange our actions into a narrative, a difficult duty considering our utter impasse in these rooms and rooms. Its method for doing so: childhood trauma. Our anti-dote: we draw pictures of Father Voice-Over's pasty body.

Some inmates speak of Father Voice-Over as though he were an angel of sorts, as if he had no body or genitals, as though he did not need a voice to speak to the inmates but rather sent his feelings straight into our brains. This seems plausible, but I also imagine him as having a pale, flaccid body and a shriveled-up penis. As soon as I start imagining this, I get paranoid. Is the father sending these images into my brain just to confuse me? I love the PA system because it seems like the act of corruption.

You have to kill Father Voice-Over as if he were your own father. As if his body was deer, says the expresident and hands me a scissor.

*

The American Dream: Several people have already awkwardly excused themselves.

In the Penal Colony: With every close-up, every fold of skin, every infected ganglia, every contaminated abdomen, every segment, every misfit and in-and-out fit, every in-fit, every in and in and in fit, every drop of blood and every drop of semen every statue glowing every shard glowing, the soundtrack gets louder.

This is how Mother Machine Gun carried me through the riots: dressed in nightingales and high on quaaludes. She had rabies she had fun she had joys in her hands she had items lodged inside her. Make no mistake about the body count: This is the Road to Joy.

It is written all over my face: I'm on the clock clock clock clock.

*

The expresident explains how to kill Father Voice-Over: When you're asked to fight a war against the Father's virgin body remember that he is not hairy and he is not alive. He is kept with the deer fetuses and the abortions. He smells like formaldehyde. If you put enough pressure on the scalpel you can cut straight through his white white skin. This is also the road to joy. But beware of tigers.

The Virgin Father's skin is very soft, almost sponge-like. The organs look like gold. As if gold had been poured down his throat in a very measured and thoughtful way. If you cut open the scrotum you will find a threadlike material. This is the fabled "dark matter" of science. There are no testicles because the Virgin Father has no testicles. His children are made from this thread-like dark matter: it enters the woman's cunt and is pulled into her water lily, which the thread then transforms into a fetus lily.

*

hares

pollutants

dissonance

silver trumpetssss

*

All day long they play the Genius Child Orchestra over the PA system. I can no longer distinguish my own words from their patricidal rants.

In their biggest hit, they envision a happening in which they descent from a helicopter to kill Lyndon Johnson by his pool at his Texas Ranch.

"That's what you need to do," says the expresident somberly.

But Lyndon Johnson is already dead and besides I'm busy, taking my "Satanic Bath."

*

"I have a warm mouth today," says the expresident with his fingers in his mouth. "That means today is the day you get rid of Father Voice-Over." Today is the day I speak in tongues. In October-tongues. The dead don't have to work. I am reminded of this truth when I look at my dead dog who sleeps in my daughter's crib with her. Small-pox dog. Black dog. Biological warfare. Mined dog. Don't touch! Don't touch! That's what we keep telling my daughter.

*

The Genius Child Orchestra has all the makings of cannibalism. The end of cinema. Black-out. Religion. I play the pounding heart. Even in the dark I can hear my pounding heart. My unborn fetus.

The shoddy reproduction of a skinned hare is my emblem.

*

The skinned hare is still my emblem. My hardcore emblem.

I want the white girls to shoot me through my childish torso.

In the incest camera: all the body parts add up to a horrible virginity, beauty, infestation, crawl flower.

In the kinomutilator we are all equals. We're all burn victims and resemble Japanese insects. It's the incest system at work.

*

My daughter is on the bang again, having accidentally used the same towel as my wife used after fucking. We think she will have twins: culture and beauty. We're giving her a special kind of tea that will induce still birth. One day I hear her squeezing in the bathroom. She's in pain. "I did it" she shouts. "I went potty. I squeezed out two squirrels." To celebrate we feed her candy worms that stink of sugar. "Can I have a real candy boy," asks my daughter with her mouth full of stinky sugar. "When you grow up," I tell her.

*

My wife doesn't think the Black Man is coming to kill me. "He's coming for the insects." But last night she dreamed my body was covered with gold. She woke up screaming. "I can still smell the burning horses."

*

Sometimes a dead child, who sometimes appear to be pregnant, appears to me in the room. She often gestures for me to turn on the TV. Somehow I think she wants to see a program about wolves. Somehow I think she may be the Starlet's ghost, even though her face is all wrong. They both have "bambi eyes" but the Starlet always wore a lot of make up, especially around the mouth. I always knew she would die. Not exactly because she drank cherry schnapps but because nobody can survive that kind of atmosphere.

*

The only figure that does not repeat is the Black Man.

Every time we try to repeat him he's something else: A lover, a criminal, a woman, a black man, a crackhead.

It's not that he's black, it's that he's black.

We see him and we don't see him.

*

The expresident begs me to kill Father Voice-Over: It's the only way to save the mansion for the infection, from the Black Man who's come to kill you, he tells me. He's serious, he tells me. I'm serious, I tell him. But I'm not. I'm telling jokes about my body. Have you heard this one: What do you call a deer stunned by bright lights? What do you call a victim of a drive-by-shooting? What do you call the sound that a fish makes when you drop it on the floor? Or the sound a basement makes when it's clammy with teenage bodies? Or what do you call an eye?

*

What should I say to make you come out?

*

The airplane refuses to get off message: "Abortion," it announces to the campus. I agree. I too am on the side of the abortion movement. It means an art that inundates the entire city with images of distorted bodies. It means getting ministers to push red-splattered baby carriages across the lawns just to get arrested in front of the television cameras.

We are powerful. We image convulsively. We handle snakes. We handle cameras with fragile models whose mouths we love because they are open. We are hysterical with vermin. We proselytize with prosthetics.

*

The Death Drive Twist: Ok, time for bang-bang in the woods. We're making a graven image. We're using opera bodies and rack bodies. Nothing too muscular. Nothing too neat about the loins. Laugh. We are photographing the farce through a bullet hole. A peeping bullet-hole called the Seraphim Theater. My wife has placed a muck-lily on my belly. That will later curdle into our fourth child, Purity. But the placenta has not yet hardened.

Daughter, get out!

Fast!

The actors are coming!

*

I'm going to join the army. But I'm going to join the other side.

*

There is a silent dog in my room that looks at me. It's the Egyptian Death Dog, strangely. It sleeps with my daughter in the crib the soldiers stole in a museum during the occupation. "My dog," says my daughter and pets the dog, which is red like a woman's pussy when the woman gives birth or struggles to give birth and is about to die. That is why my daughter calls the Death Dog "Birth Dog." For Halloween she wants us to paint her red and replace her vocal chords with strings from the balloon store.

*

Even though I know she drowned, I imagine the Starlet splattered with blood, snakes tattooed on her body. I imagine her sad but not crying. She is holding a wounded, flapping raven in her arms.

*

One of the main treatments in this mansion involves lye. That might be what is drawing the Black Man here. I think he'll use a megaphone if he kills me.

*

The soldiers patrolling the hallways have become a nuisance. They demand papers from workers and use flashlights. Their garish make-up makes them almost frightening, especially when they wield those flashlights, or when they're naked, or when they've written sayings like "Get out" or "the black death" on their torsos.

*

My wife is hard at work on prom queens.

They are still too blown-up to be life-like, too mute to have a political impact.

She's painting their lips with my semen, using a little brush, a little black brush, the kind of brush she usually uses to decorate my eye-lashes. She likes it when it looks like I'm crying.

*

I'm crying.

The expresident doesn't understand what he did wrong.

*

I have the stroke: Today I have decided to save us from the Black Man by killing Father Voice-Over.

I will make Father Voice-Over suffer like a decoy.

*

The Assassination (in Still Shots)

1. A cellular structure of strange hallways.

2. A red thread along the floor.

3. Three nurses talking about a secret attic; they don't notice me.

4. I look frightened, wild.

5. My knife is inlaid with fake diamonds.

6. I run through an exhibition hall

7. Strange anatomical wonders: snails, meat wonders, the inside of a throat, the inside of a cathedral, a mask shrunk in the rain, the S-shaped body of a thief, a proliferative crotch, blubber, language.

8. More wonders: Snow on gravestones and terrycloth.

9. Blown-up statues.

10. A vertebrae.

11. Photographs from the Civil War.

12. Spirit photographs of children.

13. I enter another corridor, this one looks like a hotel.

14. A door: "The Kingdom of Rats" is scrawled on a sign was above the door.

15. A dark room. Photographs on the wall. But Father Voice-Over is not here.

16. Photographs of interrogations on the wall: A man writhing in many poses. A man with wires. A man with a hood. A man on a mirror. A man with rubber gloves. A man with a necklace. "The mind balked," reads one caption. "They continue," reads another. "Images began to ooze like confessions," reads the third. The last one reads: "We've hit bull's eye." I recognize these images. The oriental theme: the pearls, the blue tile, the orgies, the motorcyclists, the silk.

17. Another set of images: The expresident with his breathing mask on, my daughters pregnant and feline, my wife with sperm on her, my face painted black with soot, race riots, the starlet painted silver, the actors painted red, torn paper dolls, blue opium flowers. It's a kind of plot summary.

18. The desk is strewn with instruments.

19. The on-button on the speaking machine.

20. The doorknob turns.

21. Someone walks into the door.

22. All art is pig slaughter. All writing is the shit of art.

23. I throw the knife on the floor and run back to my room.

24. The exhibition of meat wonder is a blur.

25. My wife catches me as I collapse

26. It must have been him because he was carrying an object. Objects. My objects. Like a pair of glasses or a hammer. But more like my hands. Or a cancer. The objects were ruined in the act. It hurts to kill. It hurts one's objects. I stabbed him several times and I heard his body collapse. But I did not see him clearly. It was too dark in there. The music was loud.

THE END

I wake up from the television. They're showing an extravagant funeral march: trumpets, oboes, clarinets and drums are playing a plaintive tune. I think they must be showing the funeral of Father Voice-Over.

But then a black man is carried out on a bier by twelve girls, one more nightgowned than the other. The body dressed in crimson and his turban is vermillion-orange and chrome-yellow. Around the walkway lie odalisqued ladies, their bras encrusted with diamonds. Snowy bodies, with fingers in their wounds, lie on candy-colored blankets. The birds have no teeth and the virgins have no mouthpieces. They they both make music. The graphics suggests we're witnessing the marriage of insects and transcendence, heaven and hell.

The ventriloquists are beautiful because they're wearing blue shawls. The black man is beautiful because there are flowers in his eyes and crushed seeds leaking out of his mouth.

Did I get the wrong guy? Did I kill the Black Man, I ask my wife.

No, you didn't kill anybody. Not Father Voice-Over and not the Black Man, she said.

Don't you recognize this? It's your final film with the Starlet. It's called "The Resurrection." You're playing that dark sultan character.

Just then the black man leaps up from his bier, begins to beat the floor like a fish on a boat, somersaulting, the sultan-influenced garments falling from his body, left burning on the ground.

They are playing this thing over and over on TV, says my wife. It has caused an uproar across the country. There are rumors that the Black Man killed the Starlet or that you played the Black Man all along, that the Starlet isn't dead. Or that she prophesied her own demise at the hands of the Black Man. Or that she wanted to warn us about the Black Man. It's ridiculous.

But who did I kill then in that beautiful little room plastered with photographs?

A stunt double, she replies.

*

Father Voice-Over: We ask that everyone refrain from protests in the cancer ward.

*

The corridors seem empty, as after a parade or an invasion. All the reporters have moved on, leaving garbage and random pieces of media instruments. I pick one instrument up. It's a smooth, white shell. I admire its shape but when I'm about to put it to my ear I see a snail stick out of it. I drop it in disgust and it shatters, leaving the snail there like a turd on the glossy floor. That kind of shit belongs in the cancer ward, I think to myself.

*

The doctors try to explain to me that meaning resides inside of every individual. The danger of writing is that it may ruin that self. And what would happen if we were all walking around intoxicated by beauty? "There are all these would be candy-surrealists running around ruining Art with their masturbatory Art." They have nothing, barely even books. It's all reproduction, kitsch. It's as if they were infected and keep reproducing their disease. "You can tell a surrealist from their pale skin and shivery hands," one doctor tells me. The words that keep playing in my head is "cold war, cold war."

*

The expresident needs more drugs than I do. He needs morphine and substitutions.

*

The television crews have left, sensing that the Black Man either didn't come or came and left, but the soldiers refuse to return to their barracks. In fact their pageantry becomes more and more flamboyant and disturbing: imitating horses with skeletons drawn on their pajamas, sooting their faces black and staging mock executions for the anti-abortionists, decorating certain nurses with horrible trinkets, communicating with the dead through obscene acts, smashing windows and using the shards in atrocious dances, and beating up random inmates while shouting "The Black Man did it!" Unfortunately, nobody seems able to get them back in their room. However, the soldiers tell me they've finished their poem about Baghdad. They want me to pose on a mirror for the publicity shot. Smile they scream and scream, but the make-up is too thick on my face and the tape hurts the skin on my torso. Smile they scream while my daughters give birth to insects. Smile they scream as they douse me in gasoline.

*

I am intrigued by the numbing quality of sperm.

The most romantic act is to kiss a girl who has just given you head. The lips tingle and go numb from the traces of sperm on her lips. The evolutionary reason for this is possibly similar to orgasm: a way to paralyze the female's defenses and allow impregnation, allow the foreign material to enter her womb.

My wife has been using my own sperm to keep my body from spazzing out. When I feel like I'm about to spazz she ties me down to a bed and rubs the sperm out of my penis and then rubs it on my breastcage, where it can quickly reach the heart. Then she dabs my eyelids and the inside of my thighs. Then she places a raw flower on my belly until the attack passes.

She wrecks the mirrors so I won't reproduce.

*

A foreign body is always a nonproductive body. Non-reproductive. Always reproduced. Ghastly and flat. Over-reproductive. Carries viruses in their fetuses. Generates too much poetry.

There is a travesty about foreign bodies.

They're counterfeits. We don't know how to wash them properly.

They are so bang-bang in hotel rooms.

They look horrified and come from the golden age of cinema.

That's where we learned to deal with them how to give them another voice one that sounds less awkward.

*

At one party someone made a doll of me. It was a scratch-doll. It was a charged body. There were a lot of tasers at the party. We were partying on media. Now, a child said. Blue, a child said. Now now now, a child said. I knew she must mean me.

I am supposed to build a barn in order to burn down with the pigs inside. I mean the garble-garble inside. Which belongs to the radio on account of the bite.

This is a rampant state. Everybody wants me to leave now because I failed them. Or because the Black Man is no longer coming for me, I have lost my celebrity status.

*

The Soldiers are dragging around left-over equipment from the TV crews. They want to make movies, become famous, and they think I can help them make it big. The soldier nick-named "The Poet" wants to make a movie featuring "rubber gloves and mirrors, wires and hoods"; he thinks it will be about

Beauty. A couple of soldiers want to make a movie about child abuse and wonder if they can use some of my daughters. A sharpshooter wants to make a movie about assassinations and wants me to play the role of "Viktim." One soldier who can't speak (his mouth is stuffed with pork) gestures wildly and puts his hands behind his head as if to imitate a diseased deer and when I don't understand him he starts to bang his head against the wall. Some other soldiers have to restrain him and wipe his face clean. He wants to make a movie about you, they explain, somewhat apologetically. The expresident shouts that they better clean the blood off the wall. Nobody is listening. By now most of us are watching the soldiers performing a war in the empty swimming pool.

*

The expresident needs more drugs than I do. He needs morphine and substitutions.

*

The hunt for the Black Man seems to have expanded the media landscape as the news shows chase him across the country, reporters following all the possible leads into backwoods towns and abandoned roads. And to our town. It's like the railroad was built to accommodate the gold rush. Makes me wonder if we are the gold. No, we're the buffaloes.

*

I am writing to my daughter: Sometimes when I'm drinking a cold glass bottle I think about my lover's mouth. Sometimes when I'm cutting and crying and putting out cigarettes on my arms I think about Our Mother of the Snipers and how she carried my limp body through the riot, how she wasn't my mother but more like my mother than my mother. She was gunned down in another war: the war between my heart and the head of an eagle. In those wars, my eagles always win furiously and the radio is mucky and full of holes. I'm nostalgic. Arm yourself.

*

Three soldiers are drinking Cristal in our bathtub wearing white bikinis. They claim they're there to kill horses. They want my daughters to tell them about the desert, the one where people go to invent gods. Take us there, they shout and shake my daughter. She can't speak, I explain. She's just a doll. But she can close her eyes. One blink for yes, two blinks for no, three blinks for paradise, She blinks twice, blinks twice, blinks twice as the soldiers drag her into the discolored bath water.

*

There's a rancid quality about Art that I have always thought made me susceptible to hospitalization. I'm susceptible that is to Art's rancid stench. Some people call that Cinema. I call it Influence.

*

Father Voice-Over: Your body is not that different from the fetal pig we perforate down the hall in an homage to our cultural predecessors, ghost-dancers and dandies, cake-eating beauty queens with cancer of the lips, and rat poisoners.

*

Hotel, motel, shivery inn.
Hotel, motel, sparkling skin.

*

The message I receive from the Abortionists begins: "You have become theory's effigy, you have become an inmate to your own mythologies, you are housed in your naive assertions about the birth of the clinic." It goes on from there. It is one of the most refined notes they have sent me and it came inside a condom. The spermicide caused my fingers to go slightly numb. Further, they want me to be part of a pervy new play about death. I would play the mascot. A fundamental pleasure.

I would move in the arms of a wilding holding up headlights.

I agree. I was made for this role.

*

It's been a week since I thought about nature. Nature is like fame – the photographs, the death, the deer's rotten eye.

*

We begin to hold seances to contact the Black Man. My wife enters into a trance, letting his unknown spirit enter into her body. When the shivers in her body tell us she's possessed, we ask her, "Who are you?" But she doesn't answer. Instead she stands up and begins to dance in a circle, her toes turned strangely inward, her arms going up and down in a stabbing motion, as if she were performing some kind of sacrifice. Then all my daughters – though we'd told them not to disturb us – burst into the room and, horrified at their mother's movement, rush over to her and try to stop her, hanging from her arms and legs. But my wife continues the endless sacrifice without a victim, small girls pulling at her limbs. The expresident bursts out laughing. Why are you laughing, I ask. They remind me of the war, says the expresident.

*

Teenagers are repulsive and smell bad. Some times I think they deserve nothing more than mass graves. But they look good for their age. They're all covered in milk. The age is the Age of Reason.

*

I just killed an ant on my desk with one finger.

*

The expresident thinks the Black Man on the run is not being portrayed correctly. The expresident would like to see him naked in the sand, salt in his hair, his skin almost bleached in the sun, a drowning victim of sorts.

*

The Today Show: There are fewer and fewer sightings of the Black Man in the mansion, but he's being spotted everywhere else, according to the news. Today alone, Americans have seen him at a public urinal and at a showing of the latest assassination movie. I could star in a movie like that. I've trained my whole life to be shot in the head.

*

For example the kind of trash that is thrown in mass graves.

*

My wife is not afraid of clichés. She uses the shards on my body afterwards.

*

The expresident wants to know the truth about the Starlet. What did her lips taste like? He suggests strawberry.

*

One soldier wants to make a movie about the Starlet. He wants to cover her in red orchids, he wants me to pass out in the shooting gallery, he wants to loot a museum for ceremonial daggers and stuffed hyenas, he wants to stage a romantic scene in the court room, he wants helicopters to crash, he wants to use the footage to imply the sublime, he wants the animal sounds to be real. This isn't about the real Starlet, I say, this is about Imperialism. But I've watched all of her movies, he protests with tears in his eyes.

Father Voice-Over: Get out of that shell.

THE SOLDIER'S RADIO PLAY PERFORMED OVER THE PA SYSTEM

welcome to prime time
green zone
prime time
saddam impersonator who spoke english with an english accent
a swimming pool where the girls wore bikinis so small they had to get rid of
their cunts
welcome to prime time pork
time pork zone

newspaper reporters reported to us from the outside about the outside view
of us and we watched our bodies on fox our faces were covered with bags we
wrote a manifesto a purr manifesto about cutting up men we wanted to be cut
up like men we wanted to mistreat their torsos with salt and cords and cameras
we renamed it new jerusalem bambiland land of cutting up men land of cutting
in men we named the gate the abortion murder we renamed saddam's sex
room the abortion room we named his servants quarter after muslim whores we
covered them with pork we fucked them we used pork grease we used the tickly
tips of our machine guns we took x rays we beat off with xrays in the green zone
in baghdad in new jerusalem we tripped on their bodies and the bodies of their
children and husbands we watched ourselves on fox news

we drew foxes on the whores of baghdad we painted with pork grease we were
shot we were torn to pieces in bambiland on the screen we were photographed
at the hanging we were wearing pork for the president we were naked except
for the koran and we pissed on each other in the green zone we wore art like
vampires in the light in the swimming pool we wore bikinis so small we had cut
our dicks off we were married in the vampire light we were married we were
walked down the aisle by a suicide bomber by two no three suicide bombers in
the vampire light we were naked

in the pool made of cattle bones we were washing the traces from our crotches
we were singing songs about radiation in bambiland we drank beer with bambi
we hired an architect to remake saddam's bedroom to look bombed out with
the whores of baghdad we hired an anti abortion activist to decorate the bodies

with other bodies to cover my body with fetal tattoos with tattoos of lamb fetuses with a map of the green zone with a baby in it with xmas lights in it with money on it with airplanes in it with a bankruptcy in my eyes and fosh jooks in my penis with complete strangers in bambiland in the green zone the membrane zone

in the winter palace in the shrapnel museum in the looted swimming pool in the parachute jump from the dream I posed with a saddam impersonator wearing a skeleton mask i posed next matt damon wearing a reagan mask i tore that mask into pieces and forced him to eat it while i fucked angelina jolie until she tore open and a million black bodies entered the room and we used insecticide instead of deodorant and we used pork for our bambi fucks and the frequencies were loud in the fox screen and the foxes were rotten behind the tv and reeked like iraqi children and angelina jolie reeked from children and she was torn in her pussy from me fucking her with my fox dick that also reeked of children and the hood almost strangled me it was the definition of a major metropolis

nobody left the green zone and nobody entered except journalists who brought out images and narratives to their fox stations so that we could watch our stories unfold on fox TVs while the foxes reeked in the sunlight while the bodies reeked by the swimming pool of pork and nobody left the swimming pool but we ate pork and pork and we reeked of pork and i didn't leave the green zone until mat damon showed up as the man who sold the world as the man with a dead child in the usa the man without memory the assassin with a heart of gold with a heart of candy he brought me the book of safe places for saddam and his commanders and i went to find i tortured i shot i ventured into baghdad

I went looking for the faces on the card game of most wanted heads to decapitate I looked through the pages as I walked but the pages were pornographic and did I know that today was the day of the butterfly death no I didn't so I went out with my card game and I played cards with Matt Damon I said heads or tails and then we fucked the fox-reeking angelina jolie while she spoon fed dead children with a silver spoon did i know that she had looted that from the museum that it once had belonged to a persian prince who ate from it the succulent fruits of the tigris yes I knew that because I was the one who had stolen it because i was the one who had stolen it because I was the one who loved the skull-like figure on the handle because I was the one who had used this spoon to eat pork gruel by the swimming pool I had stolen in I had stolen it I had stolen it

and then I said to matt damon show your cards and he showed me the cards the fox-reeking children and angelina jolie was rubbing pork grease on his neck and in his hair and he moaned and leaned back and reeked like rotting fox and he moaned and every card every card he had from bambiland was blank and my cards were blank and the book was blank because somebody had stolen the pornography somebody had shot matt damon full of silver bullets had shot angelina jolie's children full of gangrene and I was watching it on Fox news as I ran through the streets of Baghdad as I ran I wrote this poem on the subway as I ran I ran of pork fat and loot blood piss I followed matt damon into a house and out of a house and I was looking for saddam who was looking for matt damon who was wearing angelina jolie's face who smelled like fox rot and pork grease

in bambiland

I say to Matt Damon show me your cards but they are blank and his eyes are blank and he's painted a moustache on his upper lip it looks like a rat like a rotting rat and he is being bled by god he is saddam he is angelina jolie he says I have a million infants coming out of my torn pussy I have an infantry of infants I laugh I have been hired by fox news to tell fox news that the foxes are alive I am decapitated in the winter palace in bambiland the green zone is the heart of baghdad is the shards of baghdad green zone is a golf course where children are allowed is a rape-free zone is a rat-infested body that breeds with other bodies the green zone is not a place it's the membrane that doesn't allow any information to flow in or out doesn't allow bodies to move in our out unless they are shitty bodies bodies that don't matter don't splatter bodies that sound like glass that jump and shudder those are the bodies that are being interviewed they don't speak english they don't speak when jesus comes back this is what he's gonna look like it was the definition of a major metropolis

I sang the prologue I was ready for primetime I was singing to Mephistopheles

I was trying to warn him: Stay on the side of the light I sang. I sang: A million infants pour out of my gangrenous pussy. I saw: Men shoot me full of gangrene. I was trying to warn him to stay out of the light because he was a vampire and he wanted to hurt me fuck me rotten behind the TV so I sang: Stay in the light because I wanted him to wither like a pretty flower it was fashion I was fashion I was fashionable with my turban with my turban I was fashion I sang Jesus is going to look like Bambi when he comes out

The Sentence: The expresident has been dressed by the orphans. It looks painful. The orphans look like children. The heroes look dead but they are still breathing. The tubes look oddly like they should fit the former president's skin-tone but they do not. This is where fashion is born, in the interstice of torture and artifice.

*

The second time my wife performs the séance, she again refuses to answer our questions. "Who are you," we ask. Again, she stands up. But then she collapses on the floor. She keep getting up and collapsing. It is beautiful. Afterwards she says she only remembers the phrase "The Rose King."

*

Ugh. That's disgusting. I don't have that kind of body.

I don't have a president's body.

*

Who are we posing for today?

*

The same camera we are always posing for, the finest camera ever stenciled on the side of a hospital, the camera we use to watch the entire body – abdominal segments, veins, femurs, ears, cartilage, evil soil, rats, contusion, spilled milk, matted hair – become dangerous and muffled beneath the hood. We have dogs and hearts and lofty temples, but all those things mean nothing unless we can fit them into the photograph right now. Slaughter them later.

*

I sold America one screwy doll.

America sold me a ghost to hang in a tree: Culture.

Cough medicine: to bring me up or down.

I nail this screwy doll together for America. To find out what the uncanny can mean in an age when everything has already been a farce. I watch TV. It tells me to arrive. As if cops are beating down my door. With a sloppy animal corpse. The Rose King, I tell myself.

*

Your charming girls will survive me and my cream deaths, and I feel better knowing that, and knowing that you'll make a spine of small birds and that that spine will take my place on the bottom of a bathtub filled with cocaine and rose petals. The only knowledge is the knowledge of the skin that fails. The drone of the mirror. I'm the Rose King.

*

Back to the swiney bed.

*

Back to the swiney bed.

Pull the plug.

Pull the plug.

Pull the plug out of the shell.

Pull the slug out.

I was carried to this hospital on the arms of a thousand juvenile delinquents who sang a song about cigarette burns. And you ask me to explain myself. My fingers are numb. The projector has been kicked into pieces. It's time I describe the starlet as a torch-lit charade. It doesn't matter how the shop windows are repaired.

A pile of postcards.

*

Photograph: A black man hauled out of the rat room on a bier. The stab wounds have been circled with red ink. The flash-bulbs make it difficult to make out what they are doing to his body.

Photograph: The starvation gone horribly awry. The drainage is awful. The hit parade.

*

As my name implies, I am a sensational dancer, capable of moving gracefully while attacked with scissors or while being wrestled to the ground.

It's time I used the cutting room to decorate the Starlet, but I can't see in there. I always cut myself in there, with the foaled cancer victims and speech therapists.

The anti-abortionists leave messages under my door: "You think you're so special because you knew the starlet."

I read by the light of the spotlight outside my window.

*

You have to do something about these soldiers, the expresident snarls at me. He claims one of them is walking around in just a cod piece interrogating passers-by about the Republic. And, the expresident adds, he's not beautiful but a bit obese, pale and sweaty. What can I do, I ask. I don't know, he says, they're your soldiers. You brought them here for your theatrical interrogations of the subject.

*

I.e. I'm anorexic but I am full of fat. I'm the Real Thing, the boy with the headphones or the girl with the white out.

*

Only transcendence has been auctioned off in the rubble room. They need it for a new war. I need a new war to salvage my narrative. At first I thought I was captured because I had shot a former child star. Then I thought I was kidnapped. Then I thought I was meant to kill the voice-over. Then I thought I would dissect the virgin.

The most hilarious thing is that the place where I've been kidnapped looks just like the hotel where I was living before. The war looks the same on television and the voice is the same as in the gymnasium.

In the porno.

In the rubble room.

In the animal cords.

In the narrative death.

*

I need to take a piss.

*

The Hare: It's no use explaining pictures.

*

Photograph: A black man dressed up as the Starlet with metallic blue eye shadow and a flowing gown. Flowing in water. Drowned.

Photograph: Father Voice-Over looks angelic and wounded but perfectly alive in the spotlight, surrounded by the anti-abortion protesters, whose white gowns are smeared and splotched, whose infants are believable only as Art.

Photograph: It is shocking to see someone looking back at you from inside of the ambulance. The dress is white.

Photograph: Father Voice-Over is still waving to the crowd from his hospital window. He is still alive.

*

The dummy was bleeding from its mouth.

THE END

Joy, A History – When you've analyzed the hagiography. Pulled out the teeth. Burned the feathers. Stabbed the chest. Stabbed it again. This time with scissors. When you've interrogated gently with shards. With dogs. In the shower. Does one then know what Joy is? Joy is dead like a marine. Which is to say, Joy is proliferating.

THE END

Day #23 with my hands in a coma.

I've ransacked the Virgin Coma but I could not find my pigged-out body-body. I need it to do one more stunt for me. That stunt will be called the Torch-Light Charade. You can imagine what will happen to my pale body if I do not find the pigged-out body-body: it's the barbwire fashion show all over again.

You will throw the first stone through the window.

I walk through the gymnasium where the boys are attacking an effigy of a foreign dictator and the girls are doing cheers with pom-poms. I am enunciating the pledge of allegiance with my gym teacher's hand on my chest and my English teacher's mouth teaching me how to pronounce your name without my stutter-stutter. She wears thick red lipstick. I wear thick red lipstick.

And down the hall they are shouting my name: Eradicate! Eradicate!

Ugh. It's so cold down here in the basement it's almost so cold my hands can't type on the keyboard but things are far worse upstairs they're holding a lottery and the winner will caress the feet of a Third World Dictator.

Nobody is looking for a killer. They are looking for a star.

*

Ever since the assassination, a whole new world has opened up for me in the Shining Mansion on the Hill.

This day has stunned me with its vantage point of a whole new Road to Joy.

This new road is not lined with virgin bodies.

My wife is fiddling with the radio tuner. I mostly hear numbers and then a voice sings "rose king" or maybe "eros king" or "eros killing"…

*

I love my daughter.

My daughter loves "Candy Says" by Velvet Underground.

I'm going to watch the bluebirds pass me by.

A voice telling me to: "anorex with shells and shangri-la bodies."

I'm wide awake with a broken camera.

*

You can go, Doctor. I don't care. If you can't handle the voices, you might as well go back to being a saint with a blue wrist and an emulsified heart.

I am the center of the universe.

Only it is the center of a looted universe modeled on a model and I am fashionably colonial in my exhausted photography.

*

My wife has started to act strange, as if under a spell. Suspecting that she's cheating on me with the expresident, I climb into the closet to see what she does when I'm not there. She walks in, looks in the mirror, sets up her hair in a ponytail, takes out a box that reminds me of a small, varnished coffin and sits down. Out of the coffin she pulls different shapes made of paper and a scissor and razor blades and a lot of red pens. Come on girls, she says and all of our daughters clamor in. She sets them to work with the scissors and the pens. After a few minutes, my wife gets up pulls the top off a bunch of pens and leak their red ink into the carnage the girls are working on. The girls quickly get the ink all over. Don't eat the ink! yells my wife. It will kill you! When my wife and daughters all leave the room to clean their hands and faces, I get out and look at the carnage: a papery body of sorts, all cut and folded and stapled and smeared with red ink, several red crowns, a note of numbers and jottings with the title "Notes for the Rose King."

*

I must be some kind of revolutionary.

The discourses of fatality and wonder get a new twist when I play with myself. I hold the puppet by the golden golden strings. You represent the working class, I tell the puppet, pretending he can hear. He can't. It's so loud in here it's almost entirely silent. It's also too dark for him to read my lips. He can only see the gold glimmering when the blue light flashes through the windows. At that moment we are united by Beauty. In the darkness that ensues, I feel far away from the puppet and I think of him as a kind of weapon, one that might be used to dig a hole in my back. Into that hole: Christmas ornaments are shoved.

*

What's the difference between a doll and an automaton? I don't know, my body is strictly video.

*

The expresident wants to know what are all these soldiers doing in the mansion?
They're an army, I reply. The Anachronistic Army of the Rose King. This unsettles the expresident.
He wants me to leave the mansion.
Things would be better if you were gone, he explains.

*

Herr C,

I'm not an angel, I just crush a lot.

*

One thing must be pointed out about my relationship to the Starlet before I disappear: One does not love a Starlet the way one loves a woman or a man or a young man. One loves a starlet like a virgin loves elaborately violent codes of conduct.

*

This kind of love may seem more like hate than love.

*

In the velvet underground I am once again a virgin and I am once again soundproof.

Listen.

If you hear the sound of hares scratching on cardboard, I am watching the movie about my body. I am explaining pictures but the hares are too alive. I feel like I'm losing my daughter in a strip mall. I rinse my skin and hair and I drink champagne out of Mother Machine Gun's hands.

*

Explain: Fame, napalm, glistens, exoskeletons, waterboarding, muscular spasms, stun bodies, stunts.

In the shotdogyear of car alarms.

Explain the transportation of live cattle.

*

A pornography: The Road to Joy has been revised for a more infested audience, an audience covered in a carnage of roses.

*

The New Economy: Do not breed in this room. The results are rubbed out.

Like swans.

Visual Fever

*

The Infected Area (Against Duchamp): The gun is loaded. The nightingale is wrecked. My face is blotted out. Your face is expensive. I will finish the shooting with my retina.

*

The Road to Joy (subhorror version): The road no longer leads to Joy and I have residue on my fingers from the balloon. Now it's The Residual Road. It glimmers from opaque fluid.

*

Every fetus lining the road is also a flower with elaborate petals which I may grind up into a fluid and pour into the ampules I used to use for heroin. They were originally heating ampules. I'm being counted as a survivor, pound for pound.

*

This whole room – even the dusty lampshades, the bullet holes, the girlish bodies, even the devastating violin music and the

white dress nailed to the wallpaper – is Art. I keep taking photographs of my own body in the mirror, but it is too dark in
here, I have to light some lampshades on fire. The glare in the
mirror causes the body to look like a child's shattered body. The
background looks like velvet. But it's really Nature.

*

I was a stunt double but I was also once a teenager. Now I
am all shuddery treating translation like a séance on a bullet-
wounded body. The voice is coming from the television, the
body is littered with roses.

*

The expresident wants me to leave.
I want you to go find the Starlet's real killer, he explains.
I don't want to find him, I explain.
Well either way they're throwing you out, he explains. You and
your doll collections and your gauzes and your occult trinketry.
Why? I've done nothing wrong.
You can't pay your bills now that they won't let you teach the
soldiers any longer, explains the expresident.
I don't know where to go.
Go to Los Angeles, go to Los Angeles. That's where all the
killers live and breathe and breed horrible offspring midst the
colorful lanterns.

*

The Lust Gardens of Suffering: If you can control the shivering, you may make it to the Lust Garden of Doused Orchids and Orifices. I have a fever and my lantern is broken. It has been pierced. Inside there are many remains of stamen and scales. We have to move on to that part of my body that is still whole, still like funeral flowers.

*

Hallucination: The vehicles are not exhibited with the stamen. The ventricles are loaded.

*

We try to contact the Black Man again. This time my wife opened her eyes, looked straight at us, and said: "I'm still in hell. I'm still in hell."

I laugh as I rock on my "rocking horse." I carve the word "ham" into my thigh. This will teach my readers to take me seriously when I talk about the body as if it were a heap of texts.

*

Cough Medicine: to bring me up or down.

Back to the swiney bed.

*

I've learned to breathe with my face covered with a wet rag!

If I'm captured I won't give up the secret!

Ha, who am I kidding!? I would love to give up the secrets!

*

Bang.

Epiphany.

Haute Surveillance.

*

I tell my wife, I think the expresident wants me gone. He says
we must go to LA to find the real killer.
For once, my wife replies, I think he's right.
I think he just wants to get rid of me because he fears me.
My wife places a crown on my head.
It drips red ink on my face.

*

The gasoline fumes saturates the air, my stilts are breaking, my child listens to trilobites. The expresident has a horrified expression on his face when my wife and I fuck. My wife's belly is swollen from scorpions. She will soon give birth to a fetus. I know the path to Joy is littered with bodies and cameras.

*

When I wake up the expresident is painting my body with glitter. It's for the new beginning, he tells me. You must leave. You must go to LA. You can only save this mansion by abandoning it for a life in the movies. Go to LA. Go far away.

*

There is confetti in my hair.

*

Glitter glitter

Glitter glitter

ACKNOWLEDGEMENTS

Part of *Haute Surveillance* was published as an e-chapbook by Andrew Lundwall's Scantily Clad Press. *Boo* (edited by Nick Demske), *1913* (Ben and Sandra Doller), *Everyday Genius* (Blake Butler), *Paragraphiti* (Alireza Taheri Araghi), *Columbia Poetry Review* and *Lumina* have published excerpts from this text. Thanks to all of them for their support.

"The Soldier's Radio Play" was part of a the theatrical work "The Membrane Zone," which I performed with Tim Jones-Yelvington as part of Jacob Knabb's vaudeville show at the Empty Bottle in Chicago on April 11, 2012. Thanks to Tim and Jacob as well."

ABOUT THE AUTHOR

Johannes Göransson is the author of five books—*Dear Ra, Pilot ("Johann the Carousel Horse"), A New Quarantine Will Take My Place* and *Entrance to a colonial pageant in which we all begin to intricate*—and the translator of several more, including three by Aase Berg: *With Deer, Transfer Fat,* and *Dark Matter*. Together with Joyelle McSweeney, he edits Action Books. He blogs at montevidayo.com and teaches at the University of Notre Dame.

TARPAULIN SKY PRESS
Current & Forthcoming Titles

FULL-LENGTH BOOKS

Jenny Boully, *[one love affair]**

Jenny Boully, *not merely because of the unknown that was stalking toward them*

Ana Božičević, *Stars of the Night Commute*

Traci O Connor, *Recipes for Endangered Species*

Mark Cunningham, *Body Language*

Claire Donato, *Burial*

Danielle Dutton, *Attempts at a Life*

Sarah Goldstein, *Fables*

Johannes Göransson, *Entrance to a colonial pageant in which we all begin to intricate*

Johannes Göransson, *Haute Surveillance*

Noah Eli Gordon & Joshua Marie Wilkinson, *Figures for a Darkroom Voice*

Gordon Massman, *The Essential Numbers 1991 - 2008*

Joyelle McSweeney, *Nylund, The Sarcographer*

Joyelle McSweeney, *Salamandrine: 8 Gothics*

Joanna Ruocco, *Man's Companions*

Kim Gek Lin Short, *The Bugging Watch & Other Exhibits*

Kim Gek Lin Short, *China Cowboy*

Shelly Taylor, *Black-Eyed Heifer*

Max Winter, *The Pictures*

David Wolach, *Hospitalogy*

Andrew Zornoza, *Where I Stay*

CHAPBOOKS

Sandy Florian, *32 Pedals and 47 Stops*
James Haug, *Scratch*
Claire Hero, *Dollyland*
Paula Koneazny, *Installation*
Paul McCormick, *The Exotic Moods of Les Baxter*
Teresa K. Miller, *Forever No Lo*
Jeanne Morel, *That Crossing Is Not Automatic*
Andrew Michael Roberts, *Give Up*
Brandon Shimoda, *The Inland Sea*
Chad Sweeney, *A Mirror to Shatter the Hammer*
Emily Toder, *Brushes With*
G.C. Waldrep, *One Way No Exit*

&

Tarpaulin Sky Literary Journal
in print and online

www.tarpaulinsky.com